"Do I frighten you, Courtney?" Luke asked.

"No. Yes," she said with a sigh. "You do."

"Why?"

"You're very . . . um, male."

He smiled. "Thank you. And you're very feminine, very womanly. But I don't see why that's a problem."

"I'm just not used to having men like you around."

"Men like me? What does that mean? You're talking in circles but I know I've been insulted."

"You have oodles of women, you move in the fast lane. There's an aura about you, Luke, of . . . of sexuality. I'm just not comfortable with who you are."

"I'm just a man, Courtney. I put my pants on one leg at a time."

"Don't stand in my kitchen and talk about your pants! Especially when the pants fit the way yours do."

Luke whooped in delight. "You've been looking me over, admit it!"

"I have not! Well, just a tad," she said, feeling heat in her cheeks.

"Good, because I've been looking too. Your beautiful figure, your eyes, your lips—a man could go crazy over such kissable lips!"

She couldn't restrain a disbelieving "What?"

"I'm going to kiss you, Courtney Marshall," he said, lowering his head towards hers. "Ready or not . . ."

Bantam Books by Joan Elliott Pickart
Ask your bookseller for the titles you have missed.

WHAT ARE *LOVESWEPT* ROMANCES?

They are stories of true romance and touching emotion. We believe those two very important ingredients are constants in our highly sensual and very believable stories in the *LOVESWEPT* line. Our goal is to give you, the reader, stories of consistently high quality that may sometimes make you laugh, sometimes make you cry, but are always fresh and creative and contain many delightful surprises within their pages.

Most romance fans read an enormous number of books. Those they truly love, they keep. Others may be traded with friends and soon forgotten. We hope that each *LOVESWEPT* romance will be a treasure—a "keeper." We will always try to publish

LOVE STORIES YOU'LL NEVER FORGET
BY AUTHORS YOU'LL ALWAYS REMEMBER

The Editors

LOVESWEPT® • 190

Joan Elliott Pickart
Wild Poppies

BANTAM BOOKS
TORONTO • NEW YORK • LONDON • SYDNEY • AUCKLAND

WILD POPPIES

A Bantam Book / May 1987

*LOVESWEPT® and the wave device are registered
trademarks of Bantam Books, Inc. Registered in U.S. Patent
and Trademark Office and elsewhere.*

*If you would be interested in receiving protective vinyl
covers for your Loveswept books, please write to this address
for information:*

Loveswept
Bantam Books
P.O. Box 985
Hicksville, NY 11802

ISBN 0-553-21823-9

Published simultaneously in the United States and Canada

Bantam Books are published by Bantam Books, Inc. Its trademark, consisting of the words "Bantam Books" and the por-
trayal of a rooster, is Registered in U.S. Patent and Trademark
Office and in other countries. Marca Registrada. Bantam
Books, Inc., 666 Fifth Avenue, New York, New York 10103.

PRINTED IN THE UNITED STATES OF AMERICA

O   0 9 8 7 6 5 4 3 2 1

For the Tucson Chapter of
Romance Writers of America

One

"L and L Pharmaceuticals," Luke said into the phone. He cradled the receiver between his ear and shoulder and resumed his task of opening the mail. "Luke Hamilton? Sorry, he isn't in. Any message? . . . No? . . . Sure, call him next week. 'Bye."

"You're not in?" a deep voice said. "You must be referring to the state of your brain. I see your body sitting there."

Luke hung up the phone and scowled at the tall, dark, handsome man who sank into the chair opposite the desk.

"I'm telling you, Larry," Luke said, shaking his head as he tore open another envelope, "we don't pay Marsha enough to be the secretary for this place. When she called in sick today I said, 'No problem, sweetheart. I'll take care of everything.' I'm going out of my mind here."

His partner, Larry, chuckled. "Your phone is ringing, sweetheart."

"Hell, I've had enough of that thing," Luke said. He flipped a switch on the answering machine and a woman's voice informed the caller that L and L Pharmaceuticals was closed for the day, but if he'd like to leave a message . . . "You tell 'em, babe," Luke said, nodding at the machine. "We all went home."

"It's getting to be that time, anyway," Larry said. "I'm about ready to head home and see my gorgeous wife."

"How is my little sister?" Luke asked. "I haven't talked to her all week."

"Anne's fine, great, wonderful. She just landed a big contract to decorate a house the size of a castle."

"Good for her," Luke said, then scanned the letter in his hand. "I wonder what this is?" he muttered. "Oh, well." He dropped the letter on top of the teetering stack of papers in a wire basket on Marsha's desk and reached for another envelope. "You could help me here, you know."

"I'd hate to disrupt your system. So, it's Friday. Big date? Luke, you just threw a check into the wastebasket."

"Ah, hell." He reached into the basket to retrieve the check. "That's it, I quit. I really think we should give Marsha a raise."

"Go ahead," Larry said, shrugging. "Since she just got married, I imagine it would come in handy."

"Oh, damn." Luke slouched back in his chair. "I nearly forgot. I have to take some work over to the woman who does extra typing for us. Marsha told me that on the phone this morning." He picked up a large manila envelope and read the name written across the back. "Courtney Marshall."

"How's that working out," Larry asked, "having the overload done outside?"

"Marsha is pleased. Says this woman is fast and accurate, and she has the same word processor Marsha uses here. This Courtney Marshall lives near Marsha, so it's easy for Marsha to swing by and drop off the stuff, then pick it up."

"Want Anne and me to take it over tonight? We could go for a drive later, if you have a date."

"No, I'll go home and change out of this suit, then head out there."

"No date, Lucas? My, my, you're slipping."

"Wasn't in the mood," Luke said, shrugging as he got to his feet. "I plan on spending a quiet weekend relaxing, playing a little racquet ball, maybe working out at the gym."

"But no women?" Larry raised his dark eyebrows. "Are you over the hill now that you're thirty-five? Was that birthday you celebrated last week the turning point of your sex life?"

"Stuff it, Dawson. You'll be thirty-five in a month or so. Don't get too mouthy, because your day is coming. Go home and bug Anne. You're getting on my nerves."

Larry laughed and stood up. "Well, see ya. Have a good weekend. It sounds boring as hell, but to each his own."

"Tell Anne hello for me."

"Yep. 'Bye."

" 'Bye."

After Larry left, Luke looked around the attractive reception area. It boasted deep-piled carpeting and expensive furniture. L and L—for Larry and Luke— Pharmaceuticals was first rate and doing well. He and Larry were a good team, Luke thought, and glanced down at Marsha's desk.

With a snort of disgust and a shake of his head, he scooped the papers into a lopsided stack, then picked up the manila envelope and left the office.

Luke drove his low-slung sports car with relaxed expertise through the heavy traffic. His sprawling ranch house was several blocks inland from the beaches of Carmel, in contrast to Anne and Larry's house, which sat directly on the edge of their beach-front property. Luke liked the ocean, but didn't need to see it on a daily basis after having done a stint in the Navy with Larry years before.

At home Luke changed into faded jeans and a burgundy-colored sweater, and wasted no time in returning to his car. Dusk came early in February, and he had no desire to spend hours trying to locate Courtney Marshall's house in the dark.

As Luke drove, he thought again of his plans—or lack of them—for the weekend. He'd told Larry he hadn't been in the mood to spend Friday and Saturday night with a woman, and it was true. He'd idly flipped through his little black book at the first of the week, and mentally pictured each of the women listed. The inventory had held no appeal.

Luke didn't know why, but he suddenly just wanted no part of the swinging singles scene. Well, everyone needed a break in routine, he decided. And it sure as hell had nothing to do with the fact that he'd turned thirty-five. Thirty-five was a good age. There was nothing wrong with being thirty-five. Next weekend he'd make up for lost time, and really do up the town with a sexy lady.

Luke frowned as he stopped at a red light. He sure hoped he worked up some enthusiasm for said sexy lady by next weekend. At the moment the whole thing sounded grim. An ongoing boring, stale rerun of every weekend for the past several years. What in the hell was wrong with him? Okay, so he needed a quiet weekend, for a change, but the overall picture of his social life and sex life shouldn't have been *that* disturbing.

Oh, good Lord, he thought suddenly, his hands tightening on the steering wheel. Was he entering a mid-life crisis? Were his hormones freaking out, or something? No, that was crazy. But why did he have a hollow feeling in the pit of his stomach when he viewed his life, as though something were missing, creating a void? A hazy, chilly void.

"Forget it," he muttered. The knot in his gut was due to the fact that he was starving. He'd drop the stuff off with this Courtney woman, then go have dinner somewhere. Alone? Yes, alone. That was no problem.

"Hell."

Luke shoved his thoughts into a dark corner of his mind and slowed his speed as he drove into the residential area where Courtney Marshall lived. The modest two-story homes had fairly-good-size front lawns, which were as well kept as the homes themselves. Some of the houses were showing signs of wear, but the neighborhood was neat, clean, and welcoming.

Luke glanced at the envelope to check the address, turned left, then doubled back and found the right street a block in the other direction. He drove at a crawl, leaning over the wheel to get a glimpse of the numbers painted on the mailboxes. When he reached Courtney Marshall's house, he pulled up to the curb and absently turned off the ignition as he stared at the house. His gaze flickered to the neatly kept yard to the left, then to the right, then back to Courtney Marshall's lawn.

It was a jungle. There were gold and yellow California poppies growing a foot high across the entire yard. Politely referred to as wild flowers, they were actually brightly colored weeds that grew in abundance along the highways and open, neglected fields. The Marshalls' neighbors must be having a fit, he thought. This place was obviously lacking in tender, loving care.

Luke shrugged, picked up the envelope, and swung out of the car. As he walked up the driveway he noticed the paint on the house was showing the first signs of cracking and peeling. He absently decided it would look like hell after another summer of baking under the California sun. It was, however, none of his business, and he knocked on the screen door.

The inside wood door was swung open, but Luke didn't see anyone.

"Hi," a small voice said.

"Oh, hello," Luke said, his gaze dropping to find a dark-haired boy about five or six years old staring up at him. "Is your mother home?"

"Yeah, but she's under the sink."

"Under the sink," Luke repeated slowly. "Has she been under there very long?"

"Guess so," the boy said, shrugging.

"Do you expect her to come out soon?"

"Don't know," he said, and shrugged again.

"Right. Well, could you tell her that someone from L and L is here to see her?"

" 'Kay. Mom," the boy shrieked, causing Luke to cringe, "someone from hell and hell is here."

"L and L," Luke said, frowning. "Look, go to wher-ever the sink is and tell her. No sense screaming the roof down."

" 'Kay," the boy said, and took off at a run.

"Hell and hell?" Luke repeated, chuckling. "That ought to make a real hit with his Mom."

He glanced over his shoulder at the front yard, wondering if he'd imagined the bright, weed-filled expanse. But it was still there, the yellow and gold poppies swaying in the breeze. They were pretty flowers, he supposed, but they looked really tacky in that setting. Wild flowers belonged in the wild, not in the front yard of a residential neighborhood. Hadn't these people ever heard of a lawn mower?

The little boy came charging back to the door at full speed.

" 'Kay," he said, standing on tiptoe to unlatch the screen. "My mom says you can come in, Marsha. How come your mommy named you Marsha? That's a girl's name. Gross. My name is Kevin. That's a boy's name, 'cause I'm a boy. My sister is Jessica, 'cause she's a girl. Do you like having the name Marsha? *I* wouldn't."

Luke rolled his eyes, pulled open the screen door, which squeaked on its hinges, and stepped into the living room.

"Marsha isn't such a bad name," he said, "once you get used to it." His gaze swept over the room. It was spotlessly clean, except for several toys scat-tered about on the faded carpet. There was no par-ticular design motif, for the furniture was an assort-ment of various styles, colors, and ages. "Actually," Luke continued, redirecting his attention to Kevin, "my name isn't Marsha. She's sick today, so I brought this work from L and L."

"You work at hell and hell with Marsha? Oh, yeah, I remember her. She brings papers for my mom to type."

"It's L and L," Luke said, "not hell and hell. How old are you, kid?"

"Six."

"Don't you know it's against the law for six-year-old boys to say hell and hell?"

Kevin's eyes widened. "Really?"

"Yep. Lead me to the sink where your mother is hiding."

" 'Kay."

Luke cautiously followed Kevin across the room, weaving his way around and over the toys in his path. The boy led him into a cheerful blue-and-white kitchen, which had the standard appliances, a nicked and scarred walnut table and chairs, and a pair of tanned, shapely feminine legs sticking out from between the open cabinet doors beneath the sink. The feet were bare, with pink polish on the toenails, and one was tapping a rhythmic beat on the tiled floor, although there was no music being played in the room.

"Kevin?" a woman's muffled voice said, "Did you tell Marsha to come in? Ow! Dammit. Pretend you didn't hear that, Kevin. Honey, go check on Jessica. I'm really in a mess under here."

" 'Kay, Mom," Kevin said, and ran from the room.

Luke raised a hand to gain Kevin's attention as he whizzed by, but to no avail. He decided the kid had potential for the Olympic team in the future, then shifted his gaze back to Courtney Marshall's legs.

They were very, very nice. Smooth, silky, and—married! Lord, he was gawking at a married woman's legs. She was Kevin and the invisible Jessica's mother, the wife of the guy who was too lazy to mow his weeds. But, damn, those were nice legs.

Knock it off, Hamilton, Luke told himself. He should say something, let her know *he* had come from L and L, instead of Marsha. But what if she got rattled at the sound of a man's voice? She might whack her head on a pipe and get a concussion. Damn, he didn't know what to do!

"Marsha?" Courtney mumbled. "This isn't working at all. Hand me one of those rags, will you? I'll tie it around the pipe until I think of something."

Luke snatched a rag from the pile on the counter and held it by his thumb and forefinger. He inched closer to the sink and dangled it over one of the open doors, peering cautiously after it.

Sweet heaven, he thought, silently moaning. Shorts. Short shorts. Snug, pale blue short shorts, a lightly tanned bare midriff, tiny waist, flat stomach. Her hips curved beautifully, so—

"Thanks," she said. A hand flashed into view, snatching the rag, and disappeared.

Luke cleared his throat. He hadn't meant to, but he suddenly was having difficulty breathing, so he cleared his throat.

The shapely legs stiffened. A deathly quiet fell over the kitchen. Luke's mind clicked off a rapid list of ten places he'd rather be.

"I . . . I have a gun under here," the woman said, the trembling in her voice evident even through the muffled tone. "I'm going to shoot you dead as a post if you don't leave my house."

"Look, lady . . ." Luke said to her legs. "Ma'am . . . Courtney. Yes, Courtney Marshall. See? I know who you are, so—"

"You're a pervert! You found out my name! I'm

going to shoot you for sure. Get out! Get out! Get out! Oh, please, don't hurt my children. I'll do anything you ask, but don't touch my children."

"Courtney!" Luke yelled. "I'm from L and L Pharmaceuticals. I brought the typing because Marsha is sick. And I'm not a pervert, thank you very much."

"Oh," she said quietly. There was a pause, then, "I'll be darned."

Luke was insulted that she had unjustly accused him of being a pervert, but then all thought fled from his mind. The shapely legs were beginning to wiggle as she moved out from beneath the sink. Wiggle slowly, sensuously. Luke cleared his throat again.

His gaze was riveted to her, and he was unaware that he had gripped the edge of the cabinet door so hard that his knuckles whitened. He swallowed heavily as more, then more, of the smooth bare skin of Courtney's midriff came into view. Then . . . Oh, good Lord, he thought wildly. Her red cotton blouse was tied in a knot in front and, straining against the thin material, were her breasts, firm and full and . . . wiggling.

Oh, look at that throat, Luke thought. It was so slender, like a swan's, the sweet hollow at its base, begging to be kissed. Her face was next. She'd be ugly as sin. She had to be. Was there a pagan god he could call upon to make her ugly as sin?

"Hello, hell and hell," a soft voice said.

Luke felt as though he'd been punched in the gut. He knew he was staring at Courtney Marshall, but he couldn't tear his gaze from her delicate features. Her eyes were big and brown, and framed by long, dark lashes. Her lightly tanned skin was the color of a peach ready to be plucked from a tree, and her hair was a dark brown tumble of soft short curls. There was a dusting of freckles across her pert nose, and, Lord above, her lips were perfect. The bottom one was slightly fuller than the top, and they were shaped for, had been created for, kissing. Was she starting to smile? Yes, there came a smile, spreading over her face, giving him a glimpse of pearly white teeth and bringing a sparkle to the depths of her big, doelike eyes.

Luke Hamilton was a dying man.

Heat rocketed through his body, and his grip on the door tightened even more. He couldn't move as his eyes locked with Courtney's, and they stared at each other in the sudden silence.

Oh . . . my, Courtney thought dreamily. What an absolutely beautiful man. His hair was like spun gold. And that face. A master sculptor had chiseled it to perfection, then bronzed it in the sun. His eyes were a brilliant, captivating green. And his shoulders were so wide, and his broad chest did wonderful things for that sweater. The door was blocking the rest of the view, but she just knew it was spectacular. This was one hunk of stuff, this Mr. Hell and Hell.

"Hi," Luke managed to say.

And what a voice. So deep and rich, just right for a man his size. A man who was staring at her, visually peeling off her clothes, as she lay prone on the floor like some sacrificial virgin on the altar.

"Oh, heavens," Courtney said, snapping out of her trance and scrambling to her feet.

She wasn't very tall, Luke noticed. Five feet five maybe, compared to his own six feet. She'd fit next to him as though she were custom-made and—

"Mom!" Kevin yelled, running into the room.

Courtney and Luke jerked in surprise. Luke released his hold on the door, and only then realized his fingers were aching.

"Yes?" Courtney said. She tugged her blouse into place, then patted her hair nervously. She felt the heat on her cheeks, and told herself it was from the exertion of extracting herself from beneath the sink. Then she admitted she was lying. She'd definitely been flustered by discovering that an extremely handsome and blatantly virile man was standing in her kitchen. But she was fine now. Just fine.

"Mom, Jessica threw her shoe in the toilet, but I got it out."

"Who?" Courtney said. "Oh, Jessica! Your sister, my daughter. Well, that was very considerate of you, Kevin."

" 'Kay," he said, then ran out of the room again.

"He's really into running, isn't he?" Luke said, smiling.

Oh, don't smile, Courtney pleaded silently. Not a gorgeous smile like that. Not when her heart was still doing the jitterbug, and she couldn't remember who Jessica was. It was just too much to handle all at once. If he stepped out from behind that door she was going to dissolve into a puddle on the floor.

Luke stepped out from behind the door.

"Oh-h-h," Courtney moaned, rolling her eyes to the heavens.

"What's wrong?" Luke asked, concerned. "Did you hurt yourself under the sink, Courtney? I mean, Mrs. Marshall?"

He was wearing jeans, soft, faded jeans that molded like a second skin to those narrow hips, to his muscled thighs, and his . . . person.

"Call me Courtney," she said, smiling rather crookedly. "After all, we work for the same employer."

"Hell and hell," Luke said, returning her smile. He pulled the envelope from beneath his arm. "I brought the typing."

"Thank you," she said, taking it from him. "Oh, dear, Marsha usually waits until I look it over. I have a difficult time reading Luke Hamilton's handwriting. I think he has an inner wish to be a doctor. Marsha can decipher his scratchings."

"Lousy handwriting?" Luke asked, his eyebrows shooting up.

"Gruesome. Well, I'll have to muddle through, I guess."

"I can tell you what it says."

"Really? You're familiar with his handwriting?"

"Very."

"Do you mind waiting while I scan this?"

"Not at all." No wedding ring, he thought. She wasn't wearing any rings at all. Easy, Hamilton. Maybe she takes off her rings before she crawls under sinks. "I guess your husband will be home soon looking for his dinner, though." Corny. Really corny.

"What?" Courtney said, pulling the papers from the envelope. "Oh, no, I don't have a husband. I'm a widow."

"A widow," Luke repeated. "I'm sorry." No, he wasn't. Lord, he was a louse. She was so damn young to have lost her husband, and he was practically cheering at the news. Talk about a sleaze ball.

"Yes, I'm sorry, too," she said. "Why don't we sit down at the table while I look this over?"

"Has it been long?"

"Pardon me?" she asked, glancing up at him.

"Since your husband died."

"Two years. Joe was killed in a construction accident a week before Jessica was born."

"That's rough."

"It wasn't the high point of my life, that's for sure," she said, smiling.

"You're awfully young to be taking all this on alone," he said, the sweep of his arm indicating the entire house and her two young children.

"I'm not that young. There were twenty-seven candles on my last birthday cake. Anyway, we do what we have to do."

"Do you have family? You know, people to help you?"

"Joe didn't have any family. My parents retired to Florida. They wanted me to move there after Joe died, but I decided to stay here." She sank onto a chair. "Don't you want to sit down?"

"What's wrong with your sink?"

"It leaks. I bought a new washer, but I can't get it on right, I guess. It still leaks."

"Mind if I take a look?"

"Help yourself," she said, waving a hand breezily in the air. "I don't have any liberated hang-ups that won't allow me to accept assistance from a set of muscles. That leak is wreaking havoc with my water bill."

Luke chuckled and walked over to the sink. He glanced out the window, and in the gathering darkness saw that the backyard was a duplicate of the front. California poppies filled the entire expanse.

"You like poppies, huh?" he said, looking over at her.

She laughed, a light, tinkling laugh that caused a knot to tighten in Luke's stomach. She plunked her elbow on the table and rested her chin on her hand.

"Ahh, my yards," she said, shaking her head. "They defeated me. Poppy seeds are carried in the air and go nuts once they take hold. One minute they weren't there and then poof! I tried mowing the backyard so the kids could play, but the poppies ate the lawn mower."

"What?"

"It's an old push type. They gobbled it up, wound all around it so I couldn't move it an inch. I'll think of something, though. My neighbors give me dirty looks all the time. Know what I decided?"

"No, what did you decide?" he asked, smiling at her.

"That until I can get those poppies, which are considered weeds, poor things, out of my yard, I'm going to view them as my golden meadows. They're beautiful flowers, dancing in the breezes, being kissed by the sunshine, and creating exquisite golden meadows just for me."

What an incredible woman, Luke thought. What an absolutely enchanting, lovely, brave, incredible woman.

"I think that sounds just fine, Courtney," he said, his voice low.

Again their eyes met. They were a few feet apart, but it was as though they were close, so close, nearly touching but not quite. Luke felt heat shoot across the lower regions of his body, then saw the flush on Courtney's cheeks. A nearly palpable tension crackled through the air.

"I'll look at the sink," he said gruffly, then hunkered down in front of the open cabinet.

Courtney swallowed once, twice, and gripped the papers tightly in trembling hands. Good grief, what was wrong with her? she wondered. She was acting like a silly teenager, complete with a crimson blush on her cheeks. You'd think she'd never been close to a handsome man before. Granted, he went a tad beyond just handsome, and exuded a sexuality beyond any she had encountered before, but so what? He . . . He who? Lord, the sexiest man she'd ever met was lying flat on his back under her sink, and she didn't even know his name.

"No sign of your gun under here," he said.

"Very funny," she said, glancing over at him. The cupboard door hid most of him above the waist, giving a clear view of his . . . person, and his muscular thighs and calves. "I just realized I don't know your name, Mr. Hell and Hell," she said, deciding to look at the magnets on the refrigerator that held Kevin's and Jessica's art work firmly in place.

"Luke Hamilton at your service, ma'am," was the answer from beneath the sink.

What? Courtney thought, sitting bolt upright in her chair. Luke who? Who Hamilton? Luke Hamilton? Her boss with the lousy handwriting? No, he was kidding. "You're kidding," she said. "Aren't you?"

"Nope," he said, squirming out of the narrow enclosure. He got to his feet and placed a wrench on the counter. "There, you're all set. You were close to fixing it. It just needed a couple more turns."

"You're really Luke Hamilton?" she asked, staring at him with wide eyes. "Why didn't you tell me? I insulted your handwriting, for Pete's sake."

He chuckled and sat down opposite her at the table.

"For good reason, I imagine," he said.

"And you fixed my sink. Oh, this is terrible."

"Why?"

"Because you're my boss, my employer. You're not supposed to be under my sink."

"Aren't you overreacting a little? What difference does it make, as long as your sink doesn't leak anymore?"

"I'll have to think about that," she said, redirecting her attention to the papers. "I'll read this as quickly as I can. I'm sure you're a busy man."

"Take your time. I'm in no rush. Do you do typing for a lot of firms?"

"More all the time. I had a job in a bank for a while, but it didn't work out. My day-care expenses were nearly as much as I made. And, besides, I want to be here with my children, not have them raised by strangers. I invested in the computer last year and my reputation for producing error-free material is growing."

"Did your husband have insurance? I'm sorry. That's none of my business."

"Yes, Joe had insurance. I paid off the mortgage on this house with most of it. I have to earn enough for ongoing living expenses, which is a good trick. We're doing all right. Most of the time. Darn, I really wish you would have told me you were Luke Hamilton. I would have dazzled you with my professionalism, whisked you into my cubbyhole office where my computer lives, and . . . Oh, well, it's too late now. Thank you for fixing my sink."

"You're welcome."

"Mommy," a little girl said, walking into the kitchen. "Wanna cookie."

"Hello, my precious," Courtney said, lifting the child onto her lap. "It's too close to dinner, Jessica. We're going to eat soon. Can you say hello to Mr. Hamilton?"

"Luke," he said. "She looks exactly like you," he added, smiling at the little girl.

"I know. My mother gave me a stack of my baby pictures, and you can't tell which are me and which are Jessica. Kevin looks a bit like Joe, but Kevin has my coloring too. There's no mistaking the fact that the three of us belong to each other. Jessica, you play, then we'll eat just as soon as I read these papers."

"Play," Jessica said. She slid off Courtney's lap and toddled from the room on her chubby legs.

Belong to each other, Luke repeated silently as he watched Courtney concentrate on the papers. Yes, they did. There was a warmth in this house. No, it was a home. It had that special ingredient of love and togetherness that wove itself around the people fortunate enough to live here. This was some kind of woman, this Courtney Marshall.

Kevin appeared in the doorway. "Mom, I'm hungry. It's time to eat, 'cause 'Mr. Rogers' is over."

"I know, honey," Courtney said. "It won't be long now."

"Look," Luke said, "I'll just sit here out of the way, and you go ahead and feed the kids."

"Oh, I couldn't keep you waiting like that. I'll give them a piece of fruit to hold them over."

"No, I insist. I'm really not in any rush."

"Well, I . . . Would you consider sharing hamburgers and fries with us? That's what we're having. Then I'll whisk through reading these just as soon as we've eaten."

"You've got a deal," Luke said, smiling. All right! he thought. He was staying. Then he thought again. Why did he feel this wave of relief that he didn't have to haul himself out of here in the next five minutes? What an off-the-wall reaction.

"I'll put these papers in the other room," Courtney said, getting to her feet.

"Wait a minute," Luke said, bending over to retrieve a piece of paper from the floor. He glanced at it and his eyes widened.

"What is it?" Courtney asked, taking it from his hand. "Oh, that." She laughed merrily. "My list."

"List?"

"Yep. There it is in living blue ink. My list of qualifications for my next husband. I, Mr. Luke Hamilton, am on a husband hunt."

Two

"You're what?" Luke asked, staring at Courtney.

"On a husband hunt," she said pleasantly. "I'll be back in a sec and start dinner. I'd better change my clothes. It's getting chilly."

"Mind if I see the list while you're gone?"

"This? Oh, sure, here." She handed it to him. "That's just a rough draft. I need to fine-tune it, I think."

Luke watched as she hurried from the kitchen, then riveted his gaze on the list.

" 'Likes children,' " he read aloud. " 'Patient, kind, sense of humor. Reasonably good-looking, steady job, honest, handy around the house, as in repairing sinks, mowing lawns. Sex.' She crossed out sex? Why did she cross out sex? Hell, why am I reading this dumb thing?"

He flipped the paper onto the table, then drummed his fingers impatiently on the scarred wood, a frown on his face. His gaze was drawn again to the neat handwriting on the paper and he read the list once more.

Why had she crossed out sex? he wondered again. Even more, why would a woman like Courtney Marshall have to hunt for a husband? Men should be flocking to her door. No, maybe not. A lot of guys wouldn't come within a hundred miles of a ready-made family.

As for himself, Luke realized, he'd never even met anyone like Courtney before—a young widow with two small children, living in a house that was falling down around her ears as she struggled to make ends meet.

She was different, all right, this Courtney Marshall. Different and lovely, and as refreshing as a breath of fresh air. He'd never known anyone who could view yards of weeds as her own private golden meadows. She was definitely not someone he would ever become involved with, but was quite a woman just the same.

But a husband hunt? It didn't fit into the picture he had of her. It sounded cold and clinical, as if she already were a woman on the prowl. He knew it was none of his business, but he still didn't like it. What did she intend to do? Case the singles bars for likely candidates, with list in hand? Did she have any idea of how many weirdos and sickos were out there? There was a certain innocence about Courtney, despite her having been married and given birth to two children.

Damnit, what in the hell did she think she was doing?

He smacked the table with the palm of his hand and scowled. Feeling like an idiot, he read the list again. Why had she crossed out sex? He was definitely going to have a chat with Ms. Courtney Marshall.

At that moment she walked back into the kitchen. She had changed into jeans and a pink sweater, and wore tennis shoes. "Now we eat," she said. She began to pull food from the refrigerator, then glanced at Luke. "Is something wrong?" she asked. "You look awfully stern. Did you change your mind about staying for dinner?"

"What? Oh, no, of course not. I'll be glad to do my share too. Assign me a job."

She slid a cookie sheet of frozen French fries into the oven. "There isn't that much to do. This isn't a fancy restaurant. Kevin sets the table, but be prepared to find your fork on the wrong side of your plate. He gets confused sometimes. Would you like coffee?"

"Only if you're having it. Don't make it especially for me."

"No problem."

Luke stood up and walked slowly across the room. He leaned back against the counter next to the stove, where Courtney was making hamburger patties, and crossed his arms loosely over his chest. His gaze flickered over her, and he admired the snug fit of her jeans, the outline of her full breasts beneath the soft material of her sweater. She was as delectable fully clothed as she had been in her skimpy shorts and shirt.

"You eat three hamburgers, right?" she said. "You look like a three-hamburger man."

"Oh, yeah."

"Three it is."

"Courtney, may I ask you something?"

"Sure."

"Why the husband hunt?"

"In twenty-five words or less, my children need a father, a man to do special things with them that only a father can do."

"Okay, the kids need a father. I'll buy that. Hence the list?"

She shrugged, and lightly salted the sizzling hamburger patties. "You have to understand that I'm not exactly a pro at this. After all, I went with Joe as a teenager, then married him. The modern-day dating scene is foreign ground to me. Truth of the matter is, I have absolutely no idea what I'm doing. I had to start someplace, so I made the list, which needs revising, I think. But I should at least have a thought as to what kind of man I'm looking for."

"Why did you cross out sex?"

"Because it's confusing."

"Sex is confusing?" Luke asked, raising his eyebrows.

"No, the issue of sex, making love. Where are the buns?"

"What?"

"The hamburger buns," she said, glancing around. "Oh, there they are. Would you mind reaching in the refrigerator for the catsup and mustard?"

"Sure." He pushed himself away from the counter. "Go on with what you were saying."

"Where was I?" she asked, peering in the oven.

"Having confusing sex, or something. I don't see any catsup or mustard in here."

"Plastic squeeze bottles. The rabbit is catsup, the bear is mustard."

"Got it. Sex, remember?"

"Oh, well, it's just very hard for me to imagine

myself with a man other than Joe. I try to picture it in my mind, but it just won't come into focus. You see, I'm not counting on falling in love with this new husband, and envisioning making love with a man I don't love is beyond me. I have to work on that."

"Why wouldn't you love him?" Luke asked, placing the catsup and mustard on the table.

"Oh, I'd like him very much, and respect him and trust him, but . . . Well, love is just supposed to happen. I'm upsetting the natural order of things with my husband hunt, and I can't expect to have love too. I'd be honest about it. I'd never tell a man I loved him if I didn't. That wouldn't be fair. Marsha said that you date oodles of women, but surely you don't tell them all that you love them."

"Oodles of women? Marsha said oodles?"

"That was the word. We were chatting, that's all, and I asked her if she enjoyed working at L and L, what the people were like. She told me that everyone was super, that you dated oodles of women, that Larry Dawson is married to your sister, that type of thing. Anyway, I'm a bit confused about the sex part in regard to my new husband. In fact, just the dating has me muddled. The last time I dated I was still in high school. Do you sleep with every woman you take out?"

"No!"

"That's comforting. I was afraid it was a foregone conclusion these days. There's hope for me yet. I'll call the kids. Oh, dear, I forgot to have Kevin set the table. I'm not used to having anyone to talk to while I'm cooking, but I enjoyed it."

"This discussion is not over, Courtney," Luke said. "Not by a long shot."

"Why are you yelling?"

"Forget it," he said gruffly. "Should I put these napkins on the table?"

"Yes, please. I'll be right back with the kids."

It seemed to Luke that one minute there was nothing on the table but napkins, two plastic squeeze bottles sporting ridiculous smiling faces, and Courtney's damnable list, then in a blur of motion a complete meal was slid into place. Jessica was lifted into her high chair. The tray had been removed so that the little girl could eat at the table. That was because, Courtney said, "Jessica is so-o-o big." Jessica held her arms straight up to indicate her wondrous size. Luke told her she had nearly touched the ceiling, which brought a retort of "Did not" from Kevin.

It was, Luke decided, the most amazing dinner he had ever taken part in. Courtney kept things running smoothly with seemingly effortless ease. The conversation flowed without excluding children or adults, with even Jessica adding her jabbering two cents' worth. Courtney wiped catsup from Jessica's chin, mopped up spilled milk, gently told Kevin to get his elbow off the table, all the while listening intently to what was being said.

"My friend Freddy fell off the swing at school," Kevin said. "His knee was all bloody, and gross, and gooshy."

Luke nearly choked on a French fry.

"Thank you for sharing that," Courtney said, "but we don't talk about bloody and gooshy at the table."

"Well, it was," Kevin said. "Freddy had to have a tent shot."

"Tetanus shot," Courtney said. "Who's ready for ice cream?"

"Ice cream," Jessica said, clapping her hands.

"Me," Kevin said. "I'm going to stir it and stir it, and make it gooshy."

"But not bloody," Luke said, grinning at him.

"Gross," Kevin said, wrinkling his nose.

Luke shifted his gaze to Courtney, and they shared a smile. Their eyes held for a long moment, a very long moment.

"Ice cream, Luke?" Courtney finally asked, hearing a strange breathlessness in her voice.

"May I stir it until it's gooshy?"

"Sure," Kevin said. "Mom won't get mad, or nothing."

"I'll serve it up," Courtney said, getting to her feet. Wonderful, she thought. Her knees were trembling. Well, darn it, there was a man eating dinner at her table. No one had sat in that chair since Joe. And Luke Hamilton was no ordinary man. He was just so . . . male, and when he looked at her with those incredible green eyes of his, she melted like gooshy ice cream.

She was behaving ridiculously, she scolded herself as she spooned the dessert into bowls. There was absolutely no reason to be coming unglued simply because a virile man in tight jeans was sitting in her kitchen. There was no reason for her to have been so aware of how straight and white his teeth were when he bit into his hamburger, of the graceful way his body moved when he reached for the catsup, the way his smile spread across his face like sunshine on a cloudy day.

Still, she was that aware of him. She had a funny sensation in the pit of her stomach as though she'd swallowed a feather that was causing her to tingle inside. Absurd was the word for it, Courtney decided. She was acting absurd. Or overreacting absurd, or whatever. A man was a man, for Pete's sake.

Oh, who was she kidding? Luke was a cut above the rest, a member of that select group of the male species that was out of her league. He'd been dished out extra servings of everything. He moved with lazy grace and self-assurance, obviously comfortable with his masculinity. And he was rattling her right down to her toes.

"Here we go," she said, carrying the bowls to the table.

"Aren't you having any?" Luke asked.

"No, I don't think so. I'll start cleaning the kitchen, so I won't hold you up any longer than necessary." She snatched two plates off the table. " Enjoy your dessert."

Luke frowned as he watched Courtney scurry around the kitchen, loading the dishwasher, running water in the sink to scrub the frying pan.

Courtney was flustered all of a sudden, he mused. She'd put the rabbit-catsup container into the dishwasher, then grabbed it and nearly thrown it into the refrigerator. Was it him? Was he making her nervous? Had he done something wrong? No, he'd just eaten his dinner, which had been delicious, but he hadn't stepped out of line.

Yes, he had been watching every move she made, because she was nice to look at. But he hadn't leered or been obvious about it. He liked her smile, her laughter, the curves of her body. And he felt as though he'd been punched in the gut whenever he gazed into those great big chocolate eyes of hers. But he'd been a perfect gentleman.

So why was she whizzing through the chores like Mrs. Clean in order to get him out of here? Well, he had news for Courtney Marshall. Their discussion regarding her husband hunt and the damnable list was not over. He had to tell her to be careful, to watch out for the sleaze balls who would feed her a line, hustle her into bed, then disappear without a backward glance. She was too naive, vulnerable, and inexperienced for what was on the prowl out there.

Why was he worried about her? Luke asked himself. Hell, he didn't know. It was none of his business what she did. But, dammit, there was just something about Courtney that made him feel sort of protective. Protective? That was how Larry had felt when he'd been falling in love with Anne. Oh, no!

Easy, Hamilton, Luke thought. He was overreacting. It wasn't that strange to feel protective about Courtney. She just naturally evoked that in a man, especially here, with her two little kids, in their deteriorating house, with golden meadows for yards. He was being a nice guy, behaving like a brother.

Oh, yeah? he asked himself. Those were not brotherly thoughts he was having when his gaze skimmed over Courtney's slender but curvaceous figure, then zeroed in on those kissable lips. Lord, she had kissable lips. He wanted to feel them moving beneath his, slip his tongue inside her mouth and—

"Luke?" Kevin said.

"What!" Luke practically yelled, jerking in his chair.

"Aren't you going to stir your ice cream?"

"Oh, sure, right now. Boy, you're a pro at it, Kevin. Nice work." He looked over at the little girl. "Jessica, you missed your mouth." He wiped her chin with a napkin. "There you go."

"Do you have kids, Luke?" Kevin asked.

"No."

"How come? Don't you like kids?"

"Sure, I like kids, but I don't have a wife to be their mother."

"That's okay. We don't have a dad, 'cause he died, but my mom said we're doing fine, and sometimes kids only get one person to take care of 'em, but it's all right if the one person has two scoops of love in their heart. I'd kinda like to have a dad, though."

"Dad, dad, dad," Jessica said merrily, banging her spoon on the table.

"Maybe you'll have a dad someday, Kevin," Luke said quietly, "but if not, you should be glad you have a mom with two scoops of love in her heart."

"Yeah, she's great, my mom," Kevin said, nodding. "Do you like her? Do you think she's pretty?"

"Kevin," Courtney said, spinning around from the sink, "eat your ice cream. That special with the magician is coming on TV, remember?"

Luke smiled and looked at Courtney.

"Yes, Kevin," he said, "I like your mom, and I think she's very pretty."

Courtney felt the warm flush on her cheeks, the tingling in her stomach, the rapid beating of her heart, and told herself to stop gazing into the fathomless depths of Luke Hamilton's green eyes. But she couldn't move. She just stood there staring at him. His smile had faded, and his expression was unreadable. She assumed she was breathing, because she hadn't passed out cold on the floor, but she wouldn't make book on it. Dear heaven, what was this man doing to her?

"Potty," Jessica said.

"That's nice," Courtney said dreamily. Then, "Oh! Good girl, Jessica." She lifted her daughter from the high chair. "You should be very proud of yourself. You've kept your big-girl panties dry all day."

"Good girl," Jessica said, and ran from the room as fast as her chubby legs would carry her.

"We have very high-tech conversations around here, Luke," Courtney said, and rolled her eyes. Luke laughed.

The eerie spell that had been woven between them moments before was broken, whisked away by clattering dishes and children's voices . . . but not forgotten. Luke watched as Courtney returned to the sink; then he finished his ice cream, a frown on his face. Kevin asked his mother if he could watch TV. When she said yes, he grabbed his bowl and dashed from the room.

Luke got slowly to his feet, collected the remaining dishes from the table, and set them on the counter next to Courtney.

"It was a delicious meal, and I thank you," he said. "It's been a long time since I've had home-cooked hamburgers. I don't think I'll be able to look a fast-food burger in the face again."

"I hope you got enough to eat," Courtney said, sticking the dishes in the dishwasher. She began to wipe up the counter with quick, jerky motions, keeping her eyes averted from Luke's. "I'm not used to a man's appetite. For food," she rushed on.

"Courtney," Luke said quietly.

"There, all spiffy. I'll go get those papers and—"

"Courtney, slow down a minute."

"I imagine you're ready to escape from this zoo. I'm sure you're not accustomed to all the noise and confusion of children and—"

"Halt," Luke said, raising his hand. He closed the distance between them and placed his hands lightly on her shoulders. "What have I done to upset you?" he asked.

Courtney stared at Luke's chest. What had he done? He was there, that was what he'd done. He was causing her to behave like a flake—kept pinning her in place with those green eyes of his and throwing her totally off-kilter, that was what he'd done. And the worst thing, the ultimate awful, was that every time her gaze lingered on his sensuous lips, she wondered what it would be like to be kissed by Luke Hamilton. The rotten bum, that was what he'd done.

"Courtney, look at me."

"No," she said. Oh, super. She sounded about as old as Jessica.

"Yes," he said firmly.

Slowly, slowly she met his gaze. She nervously ran her tongue over her bottom lip, then frowned slightly in confusion at his sharp intake of breath.

"What did . . ." he started, then cleared his throat. "What did I do to cause you to flit around like a butterfly all of a sudden?"

"Nothing," she said, shifting her gaze to his right shoulder.

"Look at me," he said, increasing the pressure of his hands. "Do I frighten you?" he asked when her eyes met his again.

"No. Yes," she said with a sigh. "You do."

"Why?"

"You're very . . . um, male."

He smiled. "Thank you. And you're very feminine, very womanly. I don't understand why that's a problem, though."

"I'm not used to having a man here, that's all. It's been two years since . . . I realize I'm about to embark upon a husband hunt, but it won't include encounters with men like you."

"Men like me?" he asked, his eyes widening. "What am I? A social disease? You're talking in circles, but I can still figure out that I've been insulted. What is this 'men like you' number supposed to mean?"

"You have oodles of women, remember? You move in the fast lane. There's an aura about you, Luke, of . . . of sexuality. That's fine, great, and you're obviously very comfortable with who you are. But *I'm* not comfortable with who you are."

"I'm just a man, Courtney. I put my pants on one leg at a time, like everyone else."

"Don't you dare stand in my kitchen and talk about your pants. I can't deal with a man who stands in my kitchen and talks about his pants. Especially when said pants fit the way yours do."

Luke whooped in delight. "You've been looking me over," he said, grinning at her.

"I have not! Well, just a tad," she said, feeling the heat on her cheeks again. "Some. Sort of."

"Then we're even, because I've been looking at you too. A lot. Every inch"—his voice lowered—"of your lovely figure. And your eyes? A guy could drown in those eyes. But, Courtney, your lips are driving me nuts. They look so soft, and so kissable. Just so damn kissable."

Her lips? Courtney mused hazily. *Her* lips were so damn kissable? No joke? So why didn't he kiss them?

"I'm going to kiss you, Courtney Marshall," he said, slowly lowering his head toward hers.

Dear Lord, he was going to do it! she thought. No, no, no. Oh, yes, yes, yes!

He brushed his lips over hers, then kissed one cheek, then the other, and returned at last to claim her mouth. With gentle insistence he parted her lips to slip his tongue inside to meet hers. He shifted his arms as she moved hers; his to circle her back, hers around his neck. The kiss deepened.

Whispers of heat traveled throughout Courtney as she savored the taste, the aroma, the strength of Luke Hamilton. Intoxicating sensations coursed through her, and she welcomed them as one would a long-lost friend. She felt alive, and feminine, and aware of every inch of her own body. And aware of every inch of Luke's body. The kiss was absolutely wonderful.

A coiling knot of need twisted within Luke, and his hold on Courtney tightened as he fitted her to him, feeling her full breasts crushing against his chest. He wanted to cup those breasts in his hands, taste them with his mouth. Courtney's lips were everything and more than he'd known they would be—sweet, responsive, and totally possessed by his. This woman was heaven itself in his arms. And he wanted her, all of her.

But he couldn't have her. The message was pounding in his brain with as much force as the heated blood thundering through his veins. He had to stop kissing her. Now. This was Courtney. Vulnerable, naive Courtney, who didn't play the game or know the rules. And so he had to stop kissing her. And he would. In a minute.

He lifted his head with every intention of ending the embrace, then looked down at her. Her face was flushed, her eyes closed. Her lips were parted, and were moist, slightly swollen from having been pressed against his. She was woman, soft, sensuous, inviting woman. And never before had Luke been quite so aware of the fact that he was a man.

"Ah, hell," he muttered, and claimed her mouth again.

Courtney molded against him, relishing his almost brutal assault. His mouth was ravishing hers hungrily, urgently. She returned the kiss with an abandon that both shocked and excited her as desire swirled within her, igniting a hot flame of passion as it went. She forgot where she was, and who she was, and gave way to the sweet ache of need that was consuming her senses.

Luke, her mind whispered from a faraway place. He felt so good and tasted so good, and being held tightly in his arms was right. An empty place within her was being filled with a honeylike warmth, a smooth, rich warmth that flowed throughout her.

"Courtney," Luke murmured, lifting his head a fraction of an inch. "Can you feel what you're doing to me?"

Feel what? she thought hazily, slowly opening her eyes. Well, her breasts were crushed against his chest; then, lower than that, she could feel his—"Oh, good heavens," she said, stiffening in his arms. "You're . . . you . . . Oh, dear."

"Yeah," he said, moving her away from him. "Oh, dear."

"I'm sorry," she said, backing up farther. "I didn't intend . . . I really do apologize."

"What for?"

"Well, for . . ." Her gaze dropped below his belt. "Oh, I'm just so, so sorry."

"Courtney, quit saying that. It was a wonderful kiss, or two, or whatever. I'm not sorry we shared those kisses."

"Oh. Well, the kisses were fantastic, Luke, but I don't usually kiss men in my kitchen. Actually, I don't kiss men anywhere. I don't know what happened. You started kissing me and I was a goner. That's rather disconcerting."

"You responded to me totally."

"Yes, I did." She distractedly ran her hands through her hair. "Why did I do that? You must think I'm a sex-starved widow. Oh, how sick!"

"*Are* you a sex-starved widow?" he asked, smiling at her.

"Certainly not."

"Good. Then that means you were responding to me, Luke Hamilton, and not just reacting to any man who was kissing you. I was afraid my ego was about to take a beating. Since my body is already begging for mercy, enough is enough."

"I really am sorry about your body."

"I'll live. But, Courtney, you wanted me as much as I wanted you. You realize that, don't you?"

"Well, I—I have to check on the kids." She spun around and hurried out of the kitchen.

Luke let out a long breath, then ran a hand down his face. Whew! he thought. He was still tied up in knots. Damn, he really wanted that woman. The passion within her was just waiting to explode. But he'd be kidding himself if he believed she'd responded like that simply because *he* had been kissing her. That would be a fantastic fact, but it probably wasn't true.

Courtney was at a strange time in her life, he realized, and was breaking out of her self-imposed solitude. She was growing, and that growth was long overdue. She was too young to have been alone so long.

But, dammit, he fumed, she was headed for trouble. She was hellbent on finding a husband, which meant she was venturing out into the world to see who was available. Lowlifes, users, that was who was out there. With the reawakening of her femininity she was susceptible to the touch of a masculine hand. What if, the next time a guy kissed her, she responded the way she had to him? She'd end up flat on her back in bed. He'd kill the crumb!

"Damn," Luke said, beginning to pace the floor. He didn't like this, not one little bit. Courtney was dangerous to herself. She didn't yet know the extent of her own sexuality. She needed protecting.

So who was he? he asked himself. The original humanitarian, the good samaritan of the year? Hell, no. He wanted to make love to her, and had the ache in his gut to prove it. But he was the wrong man for her, because Courtney was right. She should have a husband and those kids needed a father. Luke Hamilton was not the man for the job.

What in the hell was he going to do? Yes, she should be married, but he hated the mental vision of her in another man's bed. He knew she needed protecting from the bozos who would try to take advantage of her, but had no idea how to keep her out of harm's way. What a mess. All he had done was knock on a door to deliver some typing, and here he was in a crazy situation that was out of control.

Luke's rambling thoughts were interrupted as Courtney walked slowly into the kitchen, her nose buried in the papers he had brought.

"What's this word?" she asked, pointing to a page.

"Projection," he said, after glancing at the paper.

"Mmm." She sat down at the table. "Could have fooled me. What's this?"

He moved behind her and peered over her shoulder. "Ratio. Courtney, we need to talk."

She tilted her head back and peered up at him. "About what?" she asked.

"Your husband hunt."

"Oh, that." She waved her hand dismissingly.

Luke settled into the chair opposite her and frowned.

"Yeah, that," he said, reaching for the list, which was still on the table. "And this list of yours. I don't think you've thought this whole thing through enough. You have to ease into the dating scene slowly, take a good look at it, discover what it's all about."

"How could I do that? A person either goes out on a date or she doesn't."

"Practice. You could practice."

"How?"

"With me," he said, leaning toward her.

She shook her head. "That's the silliest thing I've ever heard."

"Well, thanks a helluva lot. What's wrong with me?"

"Nothing, but what would be the point of going out on a date with you, when you're not the kind of man I intend to marry? Practicing moving in the fast lane won't do me any good."

"I'm being insulted again," he said, squinting at the ceiling. "I know I am."

"No, you're not. I'm simply stating facts. I don't want to be wined, dined, and seduced. I'm talking husband and father here. I have to go where those types are. Get it?"

"Where are they?" he asked, frowning. "PTA meetings?"

She shrugged. "Beats me. They're not pounding

on my door, that's for sure. Well, I know they're not entirely extinct."

"How do you know that?"

"What's this word?" she asked, pointing to the paper in her hand.

"Equation. How do you know that the good ole boys are still around?"

"What? Oh, because I have a date with one tomorrow night. My very first date of my husband-hunt campaign."

Three

"What?" Luke said, jumping to his feet. "You can't do that, Courtney. You haven't even been through basic training yet."

"I'm going out on a date, not joining the army," she said, frowning up at him.

He slouched back into his chair. "Courtney," he said, "listen to me. From what you've told me, you know nothing about the singles dating scene. It's very different these days, and you weren't even in it before, because you went steady with your husband through high school."

"True."

"You're not ready for this. Do you know that there are women who ask men out, then pick up the tab for the entire evening?"

"Of course I know that. The fact that I was tending to babies doesn't mean I was cut off from what was happening beyond my front door. I realize the women's movement has changed a great many of the old rules. That doesn't mean I have to follow them."

"Fine. Great," Luke said, crossing his arms on the table. "But you don't have the experience to spot who's who in the zoo. There are signals, unspoken messages, little things said and done, to let everyone know where you're coming from. A woman looks at me from across a crowded bar, and I read her loud and clear. If she's offering, I let her know if I'm accepting the invitation."

"That's disgusting."

"That's equal rights. She wants me, she says so."

"Her mother would be mortified," Courtney said. "Well, I'm not going to any singles bars, anyway."

"That's beside the point," Luke said, smacking the table with his hand. Courtney jumped. "The guys you're going out with probably know the score. What if you issue an invitation and you don't even realize you've done it? You could have a real problem on your hands."

"Oh," she said softly.

"Yeah, oh," he said, scowling at her. "That's why I said you need to practice."

"Luke, I am not that naive," she said, deciding to smack the table herself. "I'm not going to fall for the 'come to my place and see my etchings' routine."

He laced his fingers behind his head and stared up at the ceiling, a pleasant expression on his face.

"What kind of music do you like?" he asked, his voice low as he shifted his gaze back to Courtney.

"What? Music? Oh, mostly country-western. Then, if I'm in the mood, I listen to some classical."

"I've got a stereo system like you wouldn't believe."

He leaned forward and covered one of her hands with his. "Courtney, babe, we'll have a little wine and listen to Kenny Rogers and Willie Nelson. I've got some new tapes I'm dying to hear. Kenny Rogers crooning a love song is something to be shared. What do you say?"

"That sounds lovely," she murmured, a rather dreamy expression on her face.

"I knew it!" Luke roared.

"Oh, good Lord," she said, her hands flying to her cheeks. "You scared me to death. What's wrong with you?"

"You just agreed to go to bed with me!"

"I did no such thing, Luke Hamilton. You said . . . Then I said . . . I did not!"

"Lady"—he waggled a finger at her—"you're in trouble."

"I thought we were going to listen to Kenny Rogers," she said. "In high school when Joe and I made a date to listen to records, we listened to records, by gum."

"That was at seventeen. At twenty-seven it's background music for the good stuff," Luke said, grinning at her. "Hey, I made my intentions clear, and you accepted my invitation."

"That's despicable."

"That, Ms. Marshall, is the way it is. Now do you agree that you need some practice? Hell, you need a keeper."

"Oh, thanks," she said, glaring at him.

"Practice, practice, practice," he said. "I'll be your coach. Okay, first up. Where did you meet the yo-yo you're going out with tomorrow night?"

"He's not a yo-yo. Leonard is the physical-education

teacher at Kevin's school. I helped work on the fun-night carnival committee, and I assigned him to run the cakewalk."

"How sweet," Luke said dryly.

"A group of us cleaned up the gym afterward, then went out for coffee. A few days later Leonard called and asked me out for tomorrow night. And not to listen to Kenny Rogers tapes at his place, I'll have you know."

"Where is he taking you?"

"To a play at the civic center. Theater, Mr. Hamilton. That's classy."

"The last play I saw, all the actors and actresses were nude."

"Oh, for Pete's sake," Courtney said. "We're seeing *Romeo and Juliet*."

"Ah-ha!" Luke said. "A love story. A tragic one, at that. You'll be sad and weepy, and need comforting. Leonard's no fool. I don't like that guy."

"You don't even know him."

"Where's the list?" Luke asked. He snatched up the paper. "Let's see here. I suppose he likes kids, or he wouldn't be a teacher."

"Absolutely," Courtney said, nodding.

"Kind? Sense of humor?"

"He took charge of a dorky cakewalk, didn't he?"

"Okay, I'll give him those," Luke said. "Reasonably good-looking?"

"Yes."

"How good-looking?" he asked, narrowing his eyes.

"Reasonably. Besides, that's a subjective judgment. It's in the eye of the beholder."

"Mmm. Steady job. He flunks. Teachers starve in the summer."

"Leonard runs sports clinics all summer."

"Oh. Well, you don't know if he's honest."

"He didn't steal any of the cakes at the carnival. And as for being handy around the house, you've already fixed my sink. I stuck that on the list when the sink broke. It's not really that important."

"Maybe he has a secret drinking problem."

"Oh, Luke, for heaven's sake. Leonard is a very nice man. He's been divorced for five years and—"

"Why?"

"Why what?"

"Why is he divorced? What did he do to Mrs. Leonard, that poor little thing?"

"Mrs. Leonard took their savings and joined a commune to find herself. She's still looking. They had no children, Leonard is thirty-eight, and plans to teach until retirement. There. He's a fine, upstanding citizen of the community."

"Mmm."

"Mommy," Jessica said, coming into the room. She leaned her head on Courtney's knee and stuck her thumb in her mouth.

"Such a sleepy girl," Courtney said. "I have to give her a bath and get her to bed, Luke."

"I'll shove off, then," he said, getting to his feet.

Courtney stood up and lifted Jessica onto her hip. The little girl rested her head on Courtney's shoulder.

"You sure look alike," Luke said quietly. "Two lovely ladies."

"Thank you," Courtney said, smiling. "I'll walk you to the door."

In the living room, Luke called good night to Kevin.

" 'Bye, Luke," Kevin said. "You gonna come see us again?"

"Maybe. Be a good boy for your mom."

At the front door, Courtney shifted the heavy toddler high on her hip and looked up at Luke.

"Thanks for dinner," he said, "and . . . Be careful tomorrow night, will you, Courtney?"

"Yes. Yes, I will."

"I'll call you next week and see how it went, okay?"

"All right."

"Well, good night," he said. Dammit, he didn't want to leave.

" 'Night," she said. Oh, how sad. He was going to leave.

Their eyes met and held; then Luke lifted his hand to trail his thumb over Courtney's cheek. It was a simple gesture, a tender gesture, and Courtney thought she was going to dissolve into gooshy ice cream again.

" 'Bye, Jessica," he said, and was gone.

He closed the door quietly behind him, and Courtney soon heard the powerful roar of his sports car. Even after it had faded into the distance she just stood there, staring at the door.

"Potty," Jessica said.

"Oops," Courtney said, coming out of her fog. "Too late. That's all right, Jessica, it was my fault for standing here staring at a door like an idiot. Come on, my precious. It's bath and jammies for you. And dry clothes for me."

Courtney kissed Jessica on the forehead, then walked to the stairs. Halfway up she turned, looked at the door once more, then continued her climb to the second floor, a slight frown on her face.

Hours later Courtney lay in bed staring into the darkness. After both children were asleep, she'd gone into her small office off the living room and typed the first few pages of the work Luke had brought. It was understandable, she had told herself, that his image floated constantly before her eyes. After all, it was his handwriting she was trying to decipher.

But now, in her bed, she was having difficulty justifying her preoccupation with Luke Hamilton. There was no excuse for him to be there in her mind, smiling that smile, looking so devastatingly handsome, causing that funny, feathery feeling in the pit of her stomach.

And the kisses. Oh, those kisses. She still couldn't quite believe that she'd responded with such wanton abandon. Wanton? That was a bit much. She'd settle for abandon. Good grief, that man could kiss. Well, he'd probably had a lot of experience. In everything.

My, oh, my, she mused, what a lover Luke Hamilton would be. Such power in that magnificent body, and all of it directed toward a woman, and tempered with infinite gentleness. But Luke no doubt needed a scorecard to keep track of his conquests. He was out of her league, all right, and was definitely not husband material. Still, oh, that man could kiss.

And he was nice. He seemed genuinely concerned that she had no idea what the modern-day dating scene was like, which she didn't. She'd honestly thought he'd been talking about listening to Kenny Rogers. Oh, well, she'd get the hang of it. Luke would be proud of her.

Courtney pressed her fingertips to her lips and allowed herself to replay in her mind once more the kisses she had shared with Luke. But when desire began to churn within her, she flopped over onto her stomach, punched her pillow, and told herself to go to sleep. It was another hour before she drifted into a restless slumber.

The next sensation Courtney registered was being poked in the back. She opened one eye and looked at Kevin.

" 'Lo," she said, then glanced at the clock. "What have I done to deserve the honor of your company at seven o'clock on a Saturday morning?"

"Luke's here."

"Go back to bed, Kevin," she said, shutting her eye. "You obviously need more sleep. Luke is not here."

"Yes, he is. He's mowing the weeds in the backyard. He said I could help put 'em in trash bags later."

"What?" She scrambled off the bed. "Luke is actually here mowing my golden meadows?"

"No, the dumb weeds. Mrs. Frazier said they were a sore eye."

"An eyesore," Courtney said, hurrying to the window. She brushed back the curtains and peered out. "He's doing it. He's really doing it. That's crazy."

"I'm going to go watch him. I hope I have muscles like Luke's when I grow up." Kevin ran from the room.

"Does Luke have muscles?" Courtney said to no one, batting her eyelashes. "Why, I hadn't even noticed, honey child. Oh, ha! But why is he mowing my golden meadows?"

"Mommy! Up!" Jessica's voice floated to her from down the hall.

"The whole world is awake," Courtney muttered. "I'm coming, Jessica," she called.

A short time later Courtney was dressed in jeans and a blue sweater, had Jessica tucked on her hip, and was heading out the back door. The hum of a power mower filled the air. Kevin was sitting a safe distance away under a tree, watching Luke.

Courtney watched Luke too. His back was to her, and she was fascinated by the play of his muscles beneath his tan T-shirt. His jeans were faded to nearly white in places, and lovingly hugged his bottom, hips, and thighs.

"Luke," she said, then wondered if any sound had come out of her breathless body. "Luke," she yelled.

He glanced over his shoulder, then turned off the mower.

"Hi," he said, smiling at her.

"What are you doing? Why are you here? Where did you get that lawn mower?"

"Which one do I answer first?"

"Why are you mowing my golden meadows?"

"To impress Leonard."

"What?"

"You don't want him to think you don't take pride in your home, do you? That would never do. Oh, and the mower is mine. Anything else?"

"You can't do this."

"Why not?"

"Because you're my boss."

"Courtney, we covered that yesterday when I fixed the sink. Tell you what. You and Jessica go prepare Kevin and me some breakfast, okay? That's a fair trade. Go on. We men have a lot of work to do here. Right, Kevin?"

"Yep," the boy said, puffing out his chest.

"Right," Courtney replied, slowly blinking once before turning and going back into the house.

She'd bought his story, Luke thought, watching Courtney walk away. He was mowing her god-awful golden meadows because he was afraid she'd try to do it herself again, and it was too much of a job for her. He was going to have aching muscles himself by the time he was finished. But he was not, by damn, trying to impress Cakewalk Leonard.

"You stay under that tree for now, Kevin," Luke said. "These mowers kick things up sometimes."

" 'Kay."

Luke restarted the mower and pushed it forward. He'd had a helluva night last night. He'd tossed and turned, and thought of Courtney. He'd relived the kisses they'd shared, then groaned in frustration as his body responded to the memories. Then he'd pictured her going out with Perfect Citizen Leonard, and ended up pacing his bedroom. Courtney Marshall was driving him nuts.

Well, score one for him, Luke thought. At least he'd kept her from killing herself with these damn weeds. Lord, she'd looked sensational this morning, carrying her child, the early light pouring over her. Courtney Marshall was a beautiful woman. She wasn't his type, of course, but she was still beautiful. He'd just hang around the edges of her life for a while until he was sure she had a handle on the dating scene. It was a decent thing for him to do, would build his character a bit. Fine.

He nodded in satisfaction at his superb analytical reasoning, then began to whistle as the golden meadow began to tumble to the ground.

• • •

Courtney knew she was smiling as she prepared breakfast. And she knew it was because Luke was there. She also knew it was terribly foolish behavior on her part, but for the moment she didn't care.

She was going to allow herself the luxury of sitting across the table from him for the second meal in a row. She was going to look at him and let his sensuality weave itself around her. Just for a little while, a few stolen moments. She was going to do it because Luke made her feel alive, and feminine, and even almost beautiful.

Then, Courtney told herself, she'd come back down off her cloud of nonsense and think about her date with Leonard. Leonard was a nice man, and she was sure they'd have a pleasant evening. *Romeo and Juliet* was safe enough, tragic love story or not. Leonard could very well be an excellent candidate in her husband hunt.

Then why wasn't she looking forward to the evening? she wondered. It was her first date in years. Was she nervous? No. And she definitely wasn't excited. She was just . . . blah about the whole thing, and would have been just as content to make a batch of popcorn and stay home with the kids. Poor Leonard. She had to work on her attitude between now and then, or the man would end up wishing he'd never met her. Yes, she'd get her act together. After all, Leonard might be Kevin and Jessica's father in the future. And *her* husband? Oh, dear.

Courtney went to the back door and managed to yell loudly enough to be heard over the mower. Luke shut off the machine, swung Kevin up onto his shoulders, and headed for the house, with Kevin's delighted laughter dancing through the air. Courtney's heart did a strange flip-flop as she watched the pair approach, and she spun around to return to the stove.

"Let's wash up," Luke said, setting Kevin on his feet.

"Wash," Jessica said, holding out her hands.

"You too?" Luke asked. He picked her up. "Okay, troops, lead the way."

Courtney collapsed against the counter and pressed her hand to her forehead. First Luke toted Kevin on his shoulders, then he picked up Jessica just as naturally as you please. They all looked so good together, so—No, she had to stop thinking that way before she even got started. Luke was not a family man; he was a ladies' man. The only part of hearth and home he'd be interested in was the bedroom. Darn it, she had to concentrate on Leonard.

The meal passed in the usual organized chaos, with platters of scrambled eggs and bacon and toast being passed and all the food rapidly consumed. Luke raved about the cuisine, gave Courtney a warm smile, then retreated to the backyard with Kevin right behind him. Courtney's smile refused to disappear, and she hummed softly while she cleaned up the kitchen. She admittedly spent more time at the sink than was necessary, as the window above it afforded her a full view of the pair working in the yard.

The sun was rising higher in the sky and taking the chill from the morning air. Patches of sweat darkened Luke's T-shirt, and his hair glistened like a golden halo. He paused to sweep his arm over his forehead, and even that simple gesture fascinated her.

"My goodness," she said, shaking her head, "he is just so gorgeous."

With Jessica helping as only a two-year-old can, Courtney straightened the bedrooms, put in a load of wash, then dusted and vacuumed the living room. The toys were put away for the time being, and everything was in order. The morning had fled in a series of busy hours, and Courtney suddenly heard the sound of the lawn mower coming from the front of the house. She opened the door and looked out through the screen, and her heart started to beat wildly.

Luke had taken off his T-shirt.

Luke Hamilton, she thought giddily, was in her front yard half nude. Half not dressed. Half buck naked. Oh, heaven above, she wasn't going to survive this.

So don't look at him, she told herself.

Oh, ha! herself retorted. Fat chance of that. Her feet were glued to the floor, her gaze riveted on Luke. Oh, she was going to look, all right, and enjoy every delicious moment. The curly hair on his chest was slightly darker than the sun-streaked hair on his head. His skin was deeply tanned and wet with sweat, and his muscles were smooth and hard. His jeans rode low, oh, so low, on his hips, and a strip of chest hair narrowed and disappeared below his navel like an arrow pointing to his . . . person.

"Merciful saints," Courtney said under her breath, "it isn't fair." It really wasn't. That one man should have gotten so much of all the things that created an exquisite male specimen just wasn't fair. Especially when it knocked a certain widow for a loop, causing the heat she could feel on her cheeks, the skittering of her pulse, and the now-familiar tingling of desire in the pit of her stomach.

How in the world was she supposed to think about Leonard?

She sighed and shook her head, turned away from the door, only to gaze at Luke as a sudden thought struck her.

What she had told Luke was true. She had crossed sex off the husband-hunt list because she couldn't envision herself with a man other than Joe. But now, she realized as she stared at the perfection of Luke Hamilton's body, she could see herself being pulled into *his* arms, kissed and touched as their clothes evaporated into thin air. All of Luke's power and gentleness, his masculinity, his . . . person, would be directed at her, filling her, consuming her, making her whole once more.

Shame on you! Courtney scolded herself. Imagine her, Courtney Marshall, mentally making love with a man she didn't know, much less love. Well, there was no real harm in fantasies as long as said man couldn't read her mind. Actually, it was a positive sign that she was behaving like a twenty-seven-year-old woman, instead of a teenager.

It was, however, a bit confusing to be entertaining such thoughts. Delicious images, yes, but a tad frightening. Making love with Luke? Heavens. She was definitely getting herself all in a dither.

"Oh, Lord," Courtney said, pressing her fingers to her lips. "What is happening to me? The man is taking over my mind, my body." But not, thank goodness, her heart.

"Mommy," Jessica said. "Broke."

"What?" Courtney said, pulling herself from her jumbled reverie. "The arm came off your dolly again?

Here, I'll fix it. You poor baby, Jessica. Your mother is coming apart at the seams, just like this doll."

"Broke," Jessica said.

"That's what I'd have, all right. A broken heart if I didn't keep myself in control. Here's your dolly, sweetheart. She's all better."

"Mom," Kevin yelled as he ran to the door.

"Hello, hard-working man," she said. "What have you got there?"

"Luke said you should have these 'cause they were part of your gold—I forgot."

"Golden meadows," Courtney said. She opened the door and took the bouquet of poppies from Kevin. "Thank you," she said softly. "They're beautiful."

"They're gross weeds, Mom," Kevin said, wrinkling his nose in disgust.

"Not to me. Will you please tell Luke thank you, and also tell him that we'll have lunch in ten minutes?"

" 'Kay. I sure am workin' good, Mom. Luke said I'm the bestis partner he's ever had for doin' yards."

"That's wonderful, Kevin," she said, smiling at him warmly. "Lunch in ten minutes, okay?"

" 'Kay," he said, then ran back to the yard.

"Come on, Jessica," Courtney said, "let's go make lunch."

The poppies had a place of honor in a vase set in the middle of the table. Courtney made ham-and-cheese sandwiches, then filled one large bowl with potato chips and another with fresh fruit.

"Hands are clean," Luke said as he walked into the kitchen, "but the rest of me isn't in great shape."

She turned at the sound of his voice, and thanked the powers that be that he'd put his T-shirt back on.

"I'm feeling guilty about your tackling that mess, Luke," she said.

"We're almost finished." He sat down at the table. "Couldn't have done it without Kevin. Right, champ?"

"Right," Kevin said, appearing extremely pleased with himself.

"I really do thank you," Courtney said, sitting down opposite him.

"No problem. I needed a workout this weekend. So we both benefit from this endeavor. Those poppies look pretty in that vase."

"Weeds," Kevin said.

"Not to your mom," Luke said, not looking away from Courtney. "She saw them as golden meadows, and I think that is really something."

Oh, he was incredible, Courtney thought. Luke was so dear, so caring, and sensitive. Those poppies really were the most beautiful bouquet she'd ever received. She had a lump in her throat, her eyes were burning, and she knew she was going to cry. Luke was looking at her with such warmth and gentleness in those gorgeous green eyes of his, and she was turning into a sentimental, weepy mess.

"Courtney?" he asked, frowning. "Is something wrong?"

"What? Oh, no, no, of course not," she said, managing a weak smile. "Eat up, everyone. You must be starving."

Courtney avoided looking at Luke through the entire meal, but she could feel his gaze on her. Since she had no idea if she would grin like a fool or burst into tears, she refused to look at him. As soon as Jessica finished eating, Courtney scooped her from the high chair and mumbled something about Jessica's nap as she hurried from the room.

When Courtney returned to the kitchen Luke was leaning against the counter, his arms folded over his broad chest.

"Oh," she said, stopping abruptly. "I thought you'd gone back outside. Where's Kevin?"

"Filling trash bags. Want to talk about it?"

"About what?"

"Whatever is bothering you. You're jumpy, nervous, and you look like you're about to cry. Are you worried about your date with Leonard?"

"No, I'm not worried about Leonard."

"Hey, what is it?" Luke asked. He walked over to her and cradled her face in his hands. "Talk to me, Courtney."

She shook her head, unable to speak as a sob caught in her throat. But she was smiling as she gazed up at him, despite the tears clinging to her dark lashes.

"Ignore me," she said. "I'm being silly, and I think that bouquet of poppies is absolutely lovely."

"Ah, Courtney." He groaned, then lowered his head to claim her mouth. He kissed her gently, sensuously, as though she were made of the most delicate china.

But Courtney wanted more. She wanted to feel and taste and savor Luke. She wrapped her arms around his waist and pressed her body against his, inhaling the heady scent of male perspiration and relishing the play of muscles beneath her palms. The kiss deepened, tongues met, heartbeats quickened.

Luke finally lifted his head and drew a ragged breath.

"I'm sweaty and dirty," he said, his voice husky. "I'll get your clothes—"

"I don't care."

He wove his fingers through her silken curls and pressed her head to his chest. His other hand splayed across her back.

"I thought about you last night," he said. "I tossed and turned and thought about you. I wanted to kiss you the moment I saw you this morning."

"I thought about you, too, Luke," she whispered.

"You're supposed to be thinking about Leonard."

"I don't want to think about Leonard."

"And I don't want you to think about Leonard." He chuckled. "This conversation is nuts, Courtney." He was serious again. "Why did you look so upset before?"

She sighed. "I wasn't upset. Well, maybe I was. I don't know. I feel confused, muddled. It's nothing you can help me with, Luke. I'll have to work it through on my own."

"Are you sure?"

"Yes."

He tilted her chin up with one finger, forcing her to meet his gaze.

"Maybe I shouldn't have told you that I thought about you last night," he said, "but I did tell you, so what's done is done. As long as I'm being straight-forward, I'm also going to say that I want you—I want to make love with you."

"Oh, Luke . . ."

"Listen, okay? I can't remember ever desiring a woman the way I do you, Courtney. But I can't have you, and I know it. You need more from a man than I'm able to provide. I'm not cut out to be a husband and father. The whole thing scares the hell out of me."

"I understand," she said softly.

"Deep within me I know, I just know, that making

love with you would be like nothing I've ever experienced before. We'd be wonderful together, Courtney, but it isn't going to happen. You belong with the man you're going to marry, the one you'll come to love in time, because that's how you are, just overflowing with love."

"I don't know what to say."

"You don't have to say anything, because I'm blithering on enough for ten people. I've never met anyone like you before, someone so open, honest, giving. But I'm not taking from you. I just needed you to know that I do want to make love with you. I want it more than there are words to tell you. Are you angry because I told you?"

"Luke, no, of course I'm not."

"I'm not even sure why it was so important to me that you knew," he said, shaking his head slightly. "Maybe I'm hoping it will be easier to walk away from you now that I've said out loud that I can't have you."

"Walk away?"

"Not yet. I can't yet. I've got to be certain you've got a handle on this dating stuff first, on how to read signals and interpret unspoken messages. I'm not throwing you to that pack of wolves until you're better prepared."

"I see," Courtney said. "Well, who knows? Maybe I'll get lucky right off the bat and Leonard will fill the bill."

"I don't like Leonard," Luke said, frowning.

"You don't even know him."

"I still don't like him. Courtney, I'm going to kiss you again. Right now, this very minute. I really, really need to do that."

"And I'm really, really glad."

So he really, really kissed her.

Luke kissed Courtney with a vehemence that both startled and delighted her, and she returned the embrace with fervor. His body proclaimed his desire for her, and she rejoiced in the knowledge that it matched her own. She pushed the confusion from her heart and mind, and only felt, filling her senses with the essence of the man who held her so tightly in his arms.

"Phone," Luke said against her lips.

"Phone?"

"Ringing."

"Oh." Her eyes popped open. "The phone is ringing."

As Courtney ran from the room, Luke drew a breath so deep, it hurt. He'd done the right thing, he knew it, and he'd never in his life been so depressed. Courtney was now aware that he wanted her, but that he wouldn't seduce her into doing something she would regret. He would help her understand the complexities of the singles scene, then get out of her life. He had to, because he couldn't give her what she needed and deserved to have.

"I know I'm wrong for her," he said, looking up at the ceiling, "she knows it, everything is up front. So why do I feel like jumping off of the roof?"

"Who are you talking to?" Courtney asked, coming back into the room.

"The ceiling. I often hold in-depth conversations with ceilings."

"Fascinating. Well, my date with Leonard is kaput."

"Why?"

"That was my baby-sitter. She's sick with the flu. I'll have to call Leonard and tell him I can't go."

"Marsha has the flu too. It must be sweeping

through this area. Maybe Kevin shouldn't be out there breathing in the germs."

"If we're going to catch it, we'll catch it," Courtney said. "I hope Leonard's number is in the telephone book."

"Courtney, wait a minute," Luke said. "There's no reason for you to cancel your date."

"I'll never get another sitter on such short notice."

"You have one. I, Luke Hamilton, am going to baby-sit Jessica and Kevin tonight."

Four

Hours later Courtney sat on the edge of her bed wrapped in a towel. Out of the corner of her eye she saw her image in the mirror, and turned for a better view.

She looked like a pouting Jessica, she decided dismally. Her arms were folded tightly across her chest, her lower lip was stuck out in defiance, her eyebrows were knitted together in a frown. All she needed to do to complete her performance was to fall onto the floor and kick her feet.

But darn it, she did *not* want to go out with Leonard.

It certainly had seemed like a good idea at the time. Leonard was an excellent candidate for her husband hunt. Leonard was a very nice man. Leonard was kind, considerate, and trustworthy. But Leonard was not Luke!

"Oh-h-h," Courtney moaned, flopping backward

onto the bed. She had to stop thinking about Luke, which was rather tough to do, since the man was presently in her living room. And she had to quit reliving their kisses, remembering his touch, how it felt to be held against his strong body. The memory of his deep, husky voice telling her he wanted to make love with her had to be pushed from her mind. Somehow. "Get dressed, Courtney," she said aloud.

She pushed herself up, then whipped the towel away with a flourish. Narrowing her eyes, she critically scrutinized her naked figure in the full-length mirror.

Not bad, she decided. Not terrific, but not bad, considering she had given birth to two children. Breasts were full and high, tummy flat, with just a few, barely discernible stretch marks. Her hips, bottom, and legs were nothing to shout about, but they weren't awful, either. She wasn't fat, or particularly skinny. She was simply . . . there. So who was she trying to impress? Leonard?

"Don't be absurd," she muttered, reaching in the drawer for bikini panties and a matching bra. "There is no way on earth that Leonard is going to see my voluptuous self in the buff."

She knew she had been attempting to view herself as Luke would see her, and the realization brought a warm flush to her skin from head to toe. She really had to knock off her wanton fantasies in regard to Luke. In fact, she was going to halt all of her preoccupation with Mr. Hamilton. She couldn't handle thinking about him. Her body was going crazy, and she was teetering precariously between laughter and tears. She had to get a grip on herself. Now!

"Got that?" she said, scowling at her reflection in the mirror. "Pay attention, you dimwit." Wonderful.

Now she was talking to herself. Well, Luke talked to ceilings. And Luke was actually going to baby-sit so that she could go out with Leonard. It was a generous gesture on his part, but for some reason it wasn't sitting well. She felt slightly hurt that he was shoving her into Leonard's arms, and slightly angry, and slightly disappointed. And a whole lot confused.

It had been a strange day, she thought as she pulled on her panty hose. Luke had been there since dawn, and it had seemed natural and right that he mow the yards, share their meals, interact with her children. Kevin had practically attached himself to Luke's body, never leaving his new hero's side.

After the golden meadows had been transformed into socially acceptable yards, Luke had loaded the lawn mower into his Bronco. Then he'd asked Courtney if Kevin could ride along with him when he went home to shower and change.

Upon their return Kevin had chattered nonstop about Luke's neato house and neato hot tub and neato computer games.

And now there they were, Courtney thought, Luke, Kevin, and Jessica, sitting downstairs watching television, while she was stuck getting ready to go out with Lousy Leonard. Brother.

Her dress was a sheer cotton in varying shades of lavender and pink, with flowing sleeves that buttoned at the wrist. The waist was caught by a wide sash of the same material, and the skirt fell in soft folds to mid-calf. The stand-up collar was open at the throat, and she wore a delicate gold chain. She flicked her hair into wispy curls around her face, then stepped into black patent high-heeled shoes. Her makeup consisted of a few strokes of a mascara wand, rose lip gloss, and a dash of blush on her cheeks.

"That's as good as it gets," she said to her reflection, then marched from the room.

In the shadows at the top of the stairs, Courtney stopped, her hand tightening on the railing as she viewed the scene in the living room below. Luke was sitting on the sofa, wearing jeans and a green sweater. That sweater matched his eyes perfectly, and had nearly been her undoing when he'd returned to the house. His arms were spread along the top of the sofa, and tucked close on either side of him were her pajama-clad children.

They looked so small compared to Luke, she thought, and so safe and protected sitting by him. Their dark hair contrasted sharply with his sun-streaked golden locks, their big brown eyes so different from his green ones. But the three of them seemed so very right together, as though they belonged to one another. She wanted to complete the picture, lift Jessica onto her lap and nestle close to Luke's warmth and strength. There they'd sit. Like a family.

She was doing it again, Courtney realized. Mentally dragging Luke into a life he wanted no part of. To bed he could be dragged, but into the roles of husband and father? No. He'd been totally honest about his views on the subject, and she respected him for that. She personally felt he had a rather stinky attitude, but she did reluctantly respect it. And so, all things considered, she was very relieved that she knew she mustn't fall in love with him. It would be an exercise in futility and heartbreak, and would ruin her objectivity toward the Leonards of the world.

With a decisive nod she started down the stairs.

Luke's head snapped around. Then he pushed himself slowly to his feet and walked to the bottom of the stairs. Courtney nearly stumbled as their eyes met and held, and she planted each foot carefully in front of the other as she made her way down the steps. She stopped on the last one, eye level with Luke.

"You look . . ." He cleared his throat. "Lovely. Beautiful. You really do."

"Thank you," she said, her voice not quite steady.

The children disappeared into a hazy mist, along with the room, the house, the world. Luke slid his hand to the nape of her neck and leaned toward her. Her heart raced as he came closer and closer and— The doorbell rang.

"Oh, Lord," she said with a gasp, teetering on her spike heels.

"Damn." Luke growled, stepping back. "Romeo is here, Juliet."

She rolled her eyes, glanced quickly at Luke's stormy expression, and went to answer the door.

"Well, Leonard, hello, how are you, do come in," she said in a rush.

"Good evening, Courtney," Leonard said, stepping into the house. "I must say you look stunning."

Stunning? Luke echoed to himself. What a cornball thing to say.

"Thank you," Courtney said. "Jessica, Kevin, please say hello to Mr. Blaine."

"Hi," Kevin said, his gaze riveted on the television screen.

"No," Jessica said.

"Oh, well," Courtney said. "Leonard, I'd like you to meet Luke Hamilton, my . . . my baby-sitter. Luke, Leonard Blaine."

"You're the baby-sitter?" Leonard asked, absently shaking hands with Luke.

"I moonlight as a sitter," Luke said, "to support my aging mother and my ten brothers and sisters."

"How admirable," Leonard said, appearing slightly confused. "Then whose sports car is that outside?"

"My mother's. She's a real demon on the freeways. Courtney, may I see you in the kitchen for a moment?"

"In the kitchen?" she repeated.

"To discuss the children's snacks," he said, grabbing her arm. "Make yourself at home, Leonard. This won't take long."

Leonard just looked even more confused.

Luke nearly lifted Courtney off her feet as he hauled her across the room and into the kitchen. He shut the door behind them and gripped her by the shoulders as she stared up at him with wide eyes.

"Courtney," he said in a loud whisper, "you can't go out with that guy."

"Why not?"

"I don't like him. He's weird. He doesn't have a neck."

"What?"

"He's a short, muscle-bound box with no neck. He gives me the creeps."

"Well, he doesn't give *me* the creeps," she said, frowning at him. "What do I care if he has no neck? His neck, or lack of same, has nothing to do with the kind of man he is. He's very nice."

"Jessica and Kevin don't like him either. I could tell. Kids have natural instincts about things. They know better than to trust a loser with no neck."

"Luke, for Pete's sake, this is ridiculous. I've got to get back out there, or we'll be late for the play."

"Damn." Luke raked his hand through his thick

hair. "Do you have any mace, a police whistle, anything?"

"That's it. I'm leaving."

"Courtney," Luke said, his voice gentling, "please be careful. Promise you will."

"I'll be careful," she said, smiling. "Thank you for your concern. And thank you again for baby-sitting."

"Yeah." He lifted his hand as if to touch her, then dropped it back to his side. "Have a good time. Be careful, but have a good time."

"I will," she said, and left the kitchen.

"Ah, hell," Luke muttered, then followed slowly behind. He really didn't like No-neck Leonard. Not at all. If that scum laid a hand on Courtney he'd track him down and take him apart. Courtney should stay home. How could she go off and leave those cute little kids, who were sitting there in their pajamas, squeaky clean from their baths? Some mother. No, that wasn't fair. She deserved to go out. But not with Leonard!

" 'Bye. Be good," Courtney was saying as she kissed Jessica and Kevin. "Good night, Luke."

"Yeah," he said sullenly. "See ya."

Leonard eyed Luke warily, then hustled Courtney out the door.

Luke settled back onto the sofa and smiled down at the two children, who immediately snuggled close to him. They were A-OK kids, he decided. Courtney was doing a helluva good job of raising them. But they did need a father, and Courtney should be loved by someone who would appreciate all that she was. So here he was keeping the home fires burning while she launched her husband hunt.

He was a study in contradiction, Luke realized. He knew Courtney should have a decent man in her life, but he hated the idea of her being with any man other than himself. He, who was not interested in being a husband and father. Lord, he was a selfish lowlife. He wanted her in his bed, but with none of the strings attached.

Then again, he mused, he was feeling more than just desire for Courtney. The protectiveness was in as full bloom as her screwy poppies. And wasn't he feeling possessive, too? Yes, he supposed he was.

But he had nothing to worry about, Luke thought smugly, because he was one step ahead of everything that was taking place. He wasn't going to get hit on his blind side, the way Larry had. No, sir, he told himself cockily. He was aware of these strange new emotions he was feeling toward Courtney, and would keep them in their proper perspective. He wasn't some flaky romantic who allowed love to creep up on him and knock him over. If a man made no place for love and commitment in his life, then that was that. The love bug could move on to the next poor sap and bite him. Luke Hamilton wasn't having any.

"Nope," Luke said. "I don't want any of that stuff."

"But you said we could," Kevin said.

"What?"

"Have popcorn."

"Oh, sure, we're going to have popcorn," Luke said. "In fact, we'd better get at it. Jessica is already falling asleep here. Jessica, show me how good you're going to chew your popcorn. We don't need any stomachaches."

Jessica clicked her teeth together rapidly, causing Luke to laugh in delight.

"Excellent. You look like a popcorn-chewing rabbit. Okay, gang, popcorn it is." He stood, and swung

Jessica into his arms, then headed for the kitchen, with Kevin running on ahead. "You sure are a pretty girl, Jessica," Luke said quietly, "and you're going to grow up to be a beautiful woman, just like your mommy. Yep, just like beautiful Courtney."

Courtney had a headache. It was a dull, throbbing pain at the back of her head, and she knew it was caused by tension. She was definitely tense. She'd spent the entire play pulling her mind back to Leonard and away from Luke and the children. Mental tugs of war would give anyone a headache, she rationalized. So would faking continuous smiles. And now she was about to have pie and coffee that she didn't want. She'd earned the right to a headache.

"We were lucky to get this booth," Leonard said. "It looks like a great many people came to this café straight from the theater."

"Then we should be considerate and not dilly-dally," Courtney said, taking a big bite of pie. "Others are waiting for this table."

"Did you enjoy the play?"

"Well, I must say, Leonard, I had a rather difficult time relating to a Juliet who was in her sixties. It was a bit unconventional."

"That's a strange opinion, coming from someone who hires a beach bum to baby-sit her children," Leonard said. "Are you sure Kevin and Jessica are safe with that Luke character?"

"Well, of course," Courtney said indignantly. "I wouldn't leave my children with just anyone, you know. And Luke is not a beach bum."

"He looks like one. He's tanned in February and

drives a swanky car, which I don't believe for a minute belongs to his mother."

At least he has a neck, Courtney thought. "Luke is a fine person," she said. "It's especially good for Kevin to have a chance to be around a man."

"I agree, but not a beach bum. Your Luke could be a bad influence on Kevin."

"Luke isn't mine," she said. Darn it anyway, Luke wasn't hers. And never would be. And that thought made her headache worse. Luke had flitted into her life like the poppy seeds, creating a sudden burst of surprise, excitement, magnificence. But her golden meadows were gone now, and Luke would be gone soon too. "I really should be getting home."

"I enjoyed the evening, Courtney," Leonard said. "I hope we can go out together again soon. I'd like the opportunity to get to know Kevin and Jessica better, too."

"You would?"

"I've always wanted a family. I can see myself playing ball in the backyard with my children. I'm not getting any younger. I was very bitter about my wife's deserting me, but it's time for me to bury the past. I hope you'll give us a chance to discover what we might have together, Courtney."

The man was perfect, she thought wildly. Absolutely perfect husband material, father material, lover . . . Oh, good Lord, she didn't want to make love with Leonard. She couldn't make love with a man who had no neck.

"Will you do that, Courtney?" he asked. "Give us a chance, give me a chance?"

"Oh, well, I . . . You see, I . . . Um . . ."

"Think about it, okay? I'll take you home now. I'll feel better knowing Kevin and Jessica are no longer in the care of that beach bum. Perhaps it would be best if I arranged for the sitter the next time we go out. I really don't like that Luke."

"You don't even know him," she said, much too loudly. "Sorry," she added. "I didn't mean to yell. Men certainly are quick to form opinions about other men. Luke didn't like you either."

"Oh?" Leonard asked, stiffening and narrowing his eyes. "And why not?"

"It's not important," she said, trying to suppress a smile. It's about your lack of neck, Leonard, dear, she thought merrily. "Shall we go?"

"Wait just a minute," Leonard said, raising his hand. "I don't understand why a baby-sitter would tell you what he thought of your choice of escort for the evening."

"Oh, Luke has opinions about a lot of things," she said pleasantly.

"I'll bet." Leonard scowled. "Courtney, I'd like you to promise me that you won't hire him to sit for you again. I really don't trust him. There's just something about him, something predatory, like a cat on the prowl. I've seen his type before. They're lady-killers, playboys. Luke knows he's good-looking, and he'll use it to his advantage every opportunity he gets."

"Luke is good-looking?" Courtney said, all innocence. "My, my, I really hadn't noticed."

"My goodness, Courtney." Leonard patted her hand. "You're so marvelously old-fashioned, so trusting. You need a man to look after you, protect you from the Lukes of this world. Well, let's get going. I want that guy out of your house. I really do *not* like him."

Courtney rolled her eyes heavenward and slid out of the booth. Men, she decided, often behaved like little boys in grown-up bodies. What were Luke and Leonard going to do? Stamp their feet and stick their tongues out at each other? Or, oh, cripes, punch each other out?

Courtney waited until Leonard was driving to her house, then shifted in her seat to face him.

"Leonard," she said, "I think it would be best if you just dropped me off."

"Absolutely not. I'm not leaving your house until that beach bum is long gone in his fancy car."

"That's not necessary."

"Yes, it is. Besides, it's my responsibility to pay him."

"What?" she said, her eyes widening.

"When a man dates a woman with young children, he takes care of the cost of the sitter. I'll pay Luke, then send him on his way."

"Oh, my word, this is *not* wonderful," she said, shaking her head. "My idea is much better. You just drop me off and— "

"No."

"Oh."

Leonard parked in Courtney's driveway and walked around the car to assist her from it. She swept her damp palms along her thighs before placing her hand in Leonard's and allowing him to help her out. She swallowed a nearly hysterical giggle when she realized Luke had turned the porch light on. Her mother had done that when Courtney had first started to date, she recalled, on the premise that it kept the good-night kiss short and sweet.

"Leonard," she said, striving for firmness in her voice as they reached the front door, "I really must insist that you—"

The front door was flung open. Courtney teetered on her shoes again.

"Hello," Luke said calmly, leaning his shoulder against the doorjamb. He crossed his arms over his chest and smiled at them through the screen door. "Have fun? Well, it's nippy out there. You'd better come inside, Courtney. See ya, Leonard."

"What you'll see," Leonard said, "is yourself driving away from here. I'm not leaving until you're long gone."

"That a fact?" Luke said, his jaw tightening. "Guess again. You're the one hitting the road."

"Maybe I should warn you," Leonard said, "that I was the conference wrestling champion for four straight years when I was in college."

"Oh," Luke said, nodding. "So that's what happened to your neck. It got smashed into your square body. Shove off, Leonard."

"Don't tell me what to do, you beach bum."

"Beach bum!" Luke pushed open the screen door and stepped outside. "Who in the hell are you calling a beach bum?"

"You. I know your type."

"Listen, you neckless twit, I'm going to—Hey!"

The porch light suddenly went out, and there was a decisive click as the front door closed.

"Courtney?" Luke said, spinning around. "Uh-oh."

"I think she's mad as hell," Leonard said.

"I know she's mad as hell," Luke said.

"Now what do we do?"

"Damned if I know. The least she could have done was scream and holler, tell us we were acting like jerks. But hell, she just disappeared. Look at that— she's turning off the downstairs lights. She's going to bed, Leonard, and leaving us out here like a pair of idiots."

"She has a point."

"Yeah, I suppose she does."

"She's a classy lady."

"She sure is. Very special, very rare, very lovely."

"Yep. I'm going to be back, you know."

"Figured you would," Luke said. "I'll be around."

"Figured you would. 'Night," Leonard said, walking slowly toward his car.

"See ya, Leonard," Luke said, staring up at the dark house.

A few minutes later Luke shook his head, shoved his hands into his pockets, and strode to his car. He roared the vehicle into action and drove away.

Courtney could not remember ever being so angry. Her entire body was rigid, she was so angry. She lay in bed as straight as a pencil, hands clutched into fists at her sides, lips pursed together as she stared up in to the darkness.

She had never been so humiliated in her entire life. There they'd stood, the macho brothers, haggling over her as if she were a prize to go to the one who proved to have the most muscle power. Disgusting. They weren't men, they were brawling brats, and she didn't need them, either one. Any man, for that matter. She had two children to raise, and she wasn't taking on another little boy masquerading in a king-size body.

Cancel the husband hunt.

She'd changed her mind. The plan was off. If Luke and Leonard were examples of the modern-day male, she could do without, thank you very much. Oh,

Lord, she was furious. How dare they stand in her front yard flexing their muscles and strutting their stuff? Next year at the school carnival she was going to assign Leonard to the dunking booth. That would fix his wagon. Oh, what despicable behavior. She never wanted to see him again.

And she never wanted to see Luke Hamilton again either. She really didn't. She'd heard him drive away. He was gone. That was fine, just perfect. So what if he'd never kiss her or touch her or smile at her again? She didn't give a tinker's damn that those strong arms wouldn't pull her to that hard chest, where she could drink in the feel of him and inhale the aroma that was uniquely his.

A tear slid down Courtney's cheek.

It didn't matter one iota, she told herself hurriedly, that with the arrival of Luke at her front door had come a burst of sunshine and happiness into her life, a reawakening of her femininity, the sound of her own laughter dancing through the air.

Big macho deal that Luke was the most handsome, most masculine, most everything man she had ever met.

And if she kept talking to herself all night, Courtney thought frantically, she wouldn't have to face the fact that Luke was gone and she was going to miss him. That rotten man. She was really going to miss him.

"Oh-h-h," she moaned, covering her face with her hands. "I can't stand it. I'm so stupid, such a dumb-dumb. Some husband hunter I am. I can't do anything right." A million men out there, and she was totally preoccupied with the wrong one. Unbelievable.

Another tear fell, then another, and Courtney was just too exhausted to struggle against them. She cried until she got the hiccups and her eyes stung. Her head hurt, her nose and eyes and throat hurt, and she felt terribly sorry for herself. She mentally demanded that Luke's image get out of her bedroom. It refused to leave, and the tears started again. At last she slept, hugging her tear-stained pillow.

On Monday morning Luke was pacing back and forth across the reception area of L and L. He glanced often at his watch and the door. When the door opened, he spun around immediately.

"Marsha, you're here. Feeling okay? You look okay. Nasty stuff, that flu. Sorry your desk is such a mess. I didn't know what to do with half that junk. Want some coffee? Oh, I forgot to make it. Larry and I decided to give you a raise. So, happy raise or . . . whatever."

Marsha Stone was a tall, attractive blond of twenty-five, who was extremely intelligent and very well organized. At that moment, however, she resembled a goldfish. She was staring at Luke with wide blue eyes, and she kept opening and shutting her mouth in a futile attempt to get a word in edgewise.

"Sure glad you're back," Luke rushed on. "I see you have a manila envelope in your hand there. The kind of envelope that holds our outside typing work. Nice envelopes, those envelopes. I—"

Marsha found her voice. "Quiet!" she yelled. "I want quiet in this room."

"Yes, ma'am," Larry said, inching in the door behind her.

"You've got it," Luke said, raising his hands. "Quiet. Absolute quiet. Hear how quiet it is?"

Marsha took a deep breath, walked to her cluttered desk, and carefully set down her purse and the envelope. After another deep breath, she turned to the two men.

"Larry," she said, "I realize that Luke is your best friend, so you must be brave. He's totally deranged. We'll scour the country to find the best medical help available for him."

"Huh?" Larry said.

"Dammit, Marsha," Luke said, "that wasn't nice."

"Well, what do you expect?" she asked, planting her hands on her hips. "I walk in here fresh from my sickbed to find my boss carrying on like a blithering idiot. Thank you for the raise, by the way. I deserve it. I mean, geez, Luke, if you want to ask me about Courtney Marshall, just ask me about Courtney Marshall."

Larry sat down in a chair and rubbed his hands together. "Now we're getting to the good part," he said. "Carry on."

Luke shot him a stormy glare, then redirected his attention to Marsha.

"Did you . . . um, see Courtney this morning?" he asked, looking at Marsha intently.

"Yes. I picked up the typing you took over there Friday night."

"And?"

"And you did a nice job of mowing her yard. I thought the poppies were rather unique, though."

"You mowed some woman's yard?" Larry asked. "You've got to be kidding. What are you doing, earning money to go to camp?"

"Stuff it, Dawson," Luke said. "Come on, Marsha, give. How was Courtney?"

"She seemed . . . I don't know. Subdued, preoccupied. I met her before Christmas, when I followed up on her ad for typing, and she's always been bubbly, smiling. I asked her if she thought she was getting the flu, but she said no. I commented on the front yard, she said you'd mowed it and then I left. Now that I've seen the condition that you're in, I realize there's a lot more to this."

"Like what?" Larry asked, leaning forward. "How much trouble can a guy get into while he's mowing a lawn?"

"Well, I hung around a little longer than that," Luke said, rolling a pencil back and forth on the desk with his finger.

"Oh?" Marsha said.

"Oh?" Larry said. "How much longer?"

"It's not what you're thinking," Luke said, his voice rising. "You people have nasty minds, do you know that?"

"I'm going to have a relapse," Marsha said, sinking onto her chair. "What is going on, Luke? Courtney isn't exactly your type, what with having Kevin and Jessica."

"Who?" Larry asked.

"Kevin and Jessica," Marsha said. "Courtney's children."

"Not a word," Luke said, pointing at Larry. "Don't you say one damn word."

"How can I?" Larry said. "I'm speechless. Kids? A woman with kids?"

"I'm ignoring you, Dawson," Luke said. "Marsha, just answer one last question. You said that Courtney was subdued. Do you think she was closer to being mad or sad?"

Marsha squinted at the ceiling and tapped a finger against her chin. "Well . . ." she said finally.

"Yes?" Luke prompted.

"I don't know," she said, shrugging.

"Oh, thanks a helluva lot," Luke said, throwing up his hands. "Whoever said women understand other women," he added, stalking down the hall, "was full of bull."

Larry and Marsha burst into laughter.

Courtney sat down at the kitchen table and crossed her arms on the wooden surface. If she had a dollar for every time she'd sighed that day, she mused, she could buy a week's worth of groceries. The night had been long, the day even longer, and Jessica and Kevin would be going to bed soon, leaving the lonely evening before her. She'd moved through Sunday in a hazy blur, then resolved to face the new week with a smile and no thoughts of Luke.

But she had thought of him, and the image of his smile had taunted her. She could see him so clearly, it was as though she could reach out and touch him. She missed him. Oh, how she missed him.

"Mom," Kevin said, running into the kitchen, "somebody's knocking at the door, but I yelled, 'Wait a minute,' 'cause it's dark and you said I shouldn't open the door alone after it's dark."

"Very good," Courtney said, ruffling his hair. "I'll get it."

She tugged her red sweatshirt down over the waistband of her corduroys and crossed the living room to the door. She opened it and stared up at Luke.

"Hello, Courtney," he said quietly.

"Luke," she said, praying her voice was steady. Hello, Luke, dressed in jeans and a black sweater.

Hello, Luke, who was causing her heart to race wildly. Hello, Luke, who was absolutely beautiful. "Hello."

"I know I should have called first, but I was afraid you'd say you didn't want to see me. You can still say that and slam the door in my face, but I really need to talk to you."

"I . . . Yes, all right. Come in."

"Luke," Kevin yelled as Luke stepped into the house. "Hi. Wanna watch TV with us?"

"Lu, Lu, Lu," Jessica said, bouncing on the sofa.

"Hey, gang," Luke said, smiling as he crossed the room. He swung Jessica off the sofa and held her high above his head. Her laughter seemed to fill the house to overflowing. "How's my champ?" he said to Kevin.

"Great. In baseball today I hit the ball, Luke. I did. I got to second base."

"Way to go."

"Gonna watch TV?"

"No, I need to talk to your mom. Behave while we're out of the room, okay?" He set Jessica back on the sofa.

" 'Kay," Kevin said.

" 'Kay," Jessica said.

Luke turned to Courtney.

"We'll go into my office," she said, not looking at him. Her office was safer than the kitchen. Already there were too many memories in the kitchen.

Luke followed her into her small office off the living room. She closed the door only partway, so she could listen for the children. She turned to face Luke and slowly met his gaze.

"I came to apologize for my behavior Saturday night with Leonard," Luke said. "I was really out of line."

"You both were."

"Yeah, I know. I'm very sorry."

"So is Leonard."

"He's been here already?" A muscle twitched along Luke's jaw. "That crumb. And?"

"And what?"

"Did you forgive him? Agree to go out with him again?"

"I really don't think that's any of your business, Luke," she said stiffly.

"The hell it isn't, lady."

His hands closed around her upper arms, and he hauled her against him. Then his mouth came down hard on hers.

Five

Courtney's eyes flew wide open in shock at the on-slaught of Luke's mouth, but in the next instant the kiss gentled, and her lashes drifted down. She wrapped her arms around his neck and answered the demands of his mouth, their tongues meeting and dueling.

A groan rumbled up from Luke's chest, and he nestled her closer as the kiss intensified. She inched her fingers into his tawny hair and pressed his head harder to hers.

With trembling hands he finally moved her away from him. He started to speak, then cleared his throat and tried again. "I really am sorry about Saturday night."

"I accept your apology," she said in a wobbly whisper. She took a deep breath, then fiddled with the waistband of her sweatshirt, willing her heart to return to a normal cadence.

"Every time I kiss you, you give more, respond more," Luke said softly. "I can feel it, and it's good, so damn good. I kiss you and I don't want to stop."

"But you do stop," she said, looking up at him.

"Yes, I do. I told you how much I want you, want to make love with you, and that hasn't changed. But nothing else has changed either. I'm still the wrong man for you."

Nothing had changed? Courtney thought. Wrong. Everything was different now, because Luke was consuming her mind as well as her body. Darn it, she certainly hadn't planned on Luke's taking front-row center. She hadn't planned on Joe's dying and leaving her alone with two children to raise either, but he had. So she'd adjusted, and she did the best she could under the circumstances that had been thrust upon her.

Here she was again, she realized, regrouping, facing the facts head on. She was becoming more and more emotionally involved with a man who wanted her physically, but who had honestly stated her life-style wasn't what he wanted. So be it. Life, as she knew only too well, did not always follow the lovely scenario that a person pieced together in her mind. She would gather her strength and inner resources and accept things as they now were.

"Courtney," Luke said, "do you mind telling me what you told Leonard?"

"What? Oh, well, I accepted his apology, then said I thought perhaps I wasn't quite ready for the dating scene yet."

"You did?" he said, a smile instantly on his face. "That's great. That's exactly what I've been trying to tell you. You need to practice first."

"No, I really don't want—"

"We'll start Friday night, okay? That should give you enough time to get a sitter. We'll go out to dinner, then dancing. I'll point things out to you, clue you in as to what signals are being passed between the other people. It'll give you a chance to see what's going on, so that you'll know what to avoid doing."

"But I'm not interested in—"

"Please, Courtney? It's so important to me that you know what you're facing when you put your husband hunt back into action."

"Oh, why not?" she said, throwing up her hands.

"Great." He glanced around the small room. "Say, you've fixed this up very nicely. You picked a good computer and printer, too."

"I did very careful research before I bought them," she said, managing a weak smile.

"Do you have any games for Kevin to play?"

"Only one. They're very expensive."

"I have a bunch he could use. Some are educational; others are just plain old fun. A buddy of mine writes computer programs and gives me samples, even of kids' games."

"Well, research has shown that children's hand-eye coordination is improved even when they're playing arcade games. The one I got him is educational, but I have no objection to the others. I'm not sure you should loan them to Kevin, though. He tries to be careful, but it's so easy to destroy those disks."

"Don't worry about that," Luke said, shrugging. "I'll pick out some super stuff for him."

"Well, all right. Thank you."

Luke nodded and moved around the office, leaning over to peer at the computer and printer, then examining the titles of the books in the narrow bookcase. A desk was set against one wall, and was neat as a pin.

"Really nice," he said, walking back to Courtney. "Efficient, but cozy, homey. You have a knack for creating a very warm, inviting atmosphere. But that's part of being a homemaker, isn't it? I felt the difference in this house the first time I was here."

And he didn't want any of what it offered, Courtney thought.

"I have to get Jessica to bed," she said.

"Okay," he said, placing his hand on her cheek. "Friday night? Eight o'clock?"

"Yes, that's fine."

Luke leaned closer and brushed his lips over hers. Then he slid his hand to the nape of her neck and increased the pressure of his mouth to a hard, searing meeting of lips and tongues.

"No," he said, suddenly lifting his head. "Bad plan. I'd better not start kissing you like that again. Come on." He reached behind her for the doorknob. "Let's get out of here. This room is too intimate, Courtney. Remember that. Don't offer to show your dates this office. It's off limits."

She glared at him, then marched into the living room.

"Bedtime, Jessica," she said, forcing a lightness in her voice.

"Lu, Lu," Jessica said, standing up on the sofa and lifting her arms to him. "Piggy, Lu."

"What?" Courtney asked.

"I gave her a piggyback ride up to bed the other

night," Luke said, grinning rather sheepishly. "It wasn't dangerous. She held on so tight, she nearly strangled me."

"Piggy, piggy, Lu," Jessica said, clapping her hands.

"Oh," Courtney said. "Well, it was apparently a really fun ride."

"Can we do it again?" Luke asked.

Courtney laughed. "Which of you enjoyed it more? Yes, go ahead. I'll follow you up and tuck her in."

"All right," Luke said, holding out his arms to Jessica. "Let's go, squirt."

Jessica squealed in delight as Luke swung her onto his back and they headed for the stairs.

"I'll be down in a few minutes, Kevin," Courtney said.

" 'Kay."

"Oink, oink, oink," Luke bellowed as he climbed the stairs. "Piggyback rides call for pig noises. Say 'oink,' Jessica."

"Oink, oink," the little girl yelled.

"Oh, good grief," Courtney said, following after the pair. And, oh, good grief, they looked so wonderful together, Jessica and Luke, and Kevin and Luke, and . . . and Courtney and Luke. Dear heaven, if she didn't keep a tight rein on her heart, she could end up falling in love with this man!

After she was in her crib Jessica insisted on giving several sloppy kisses to both Courtney and Luke, then flopped onto her stomach with a happy sigh. Courtney tucked the blanket around her, then wound up a musical bear that sat in the corner of the crib.

"Good night, precious," Courtney said.

"Nigh'-nigh', Mommy," Jessica said sleepily. "Nigh'-nigh', Lu."

"Sleep well, Jessica," he said. "Dream dreamy dreams."

Courtney turned and left the room, then waited in the hall as Luke lingered for a long moment by Jessica's crib.

"She's really something, Courtney," he said when he joined her. "So is Kevin. You've done a fantastic job of raising them."

"They have a lot of growing up to do yet. My job is a long way from being over."

He nodded. "That's true. I can really understand why you want them to have a father. The interaction is different and . . . Yeah, it makes sense."

"Well, it won't be the end of the world if it doesn't happen. There are a great many single parents in the world today. I have to believe Kevin and Jessica will be all right if there's no permanent man in their lives."

"And you? Will you be all right if your husband hunt fizzles?"

The husband hunt is canceled, you dolt, Courtney thought. It was over because she couldn't think past the big lug standing right in front of her.

"If it fizzles, it fizzles," she said breezily, starting down the hall. "No big deal."

"Hold it." He strode after her and grabbed her arm. "Where's this attitude coming from? You need a man in your life, and you know it."

"Need?" she said, stopping and looking up at him. "As in a thirsty person in the desert needing a drink or he'll die? No, Luke, I don't *need* a husband in that context. I'd like a man as my partner, my friend, my lover. It would be splendid to have someone to share with, go through the good times and bad with. But I'm capable of functioning on my own and raising those children on my own. I'd prefer not to, but I certainly could do it. I am doing it, in case you haven't noticed."

"Of course I've noticed. And you're doing a helluva job."

"Let me explain something to you," she said. "My parents were concerned when I married so young. They said I never had a chance to function alone, discover who I was as a woman. Well, in the two years since Joe died, I've discovered exactly who I am, what makes me truly happy. I was meant to be a wife, a mother, a homemaker. So you see, I don't *have* to have a man to survive, but I do want to be half of that kind of a whole again."

"And you should be. You have so much to offer a man, Courtney."

"It has to be the right man, Luke," she said, tears stinging at the back of her eyes, "and he has to want what I'm offering. All of it, not just bits and pieces, pick and choose." And it wasn't going to happen with Luke. He didn't want it all.

He frowned, nodded; then they walked down the stairs in silence.

"Wanna watch TV, Luke?" Kevin asked.

"Not tonight, kiddo. I'll see you soon, though."

"You should go to Luke's and see his hot tub, Mom," Kevin said. "It's so-o-o neato."

"I'm sure it is," Courtney said.

"Wanna try out my hot tub, doll?" Luke asked, wiggling his eyebrows.

"Not on your life, buster."

"You're learning, Courtney," he said, laughing. "I'm such a great coach. See ya, Kevin."

" 'Bye, Luke."

"Good night, Courtney. Thanks for accepting my apology. I'll see you Friday night."

"All right."

They looked at each other for a long, long moment, and Courtney's knees began to tremble. Then Luke turned and left the house, closing the door quietly behind him. A soft smile formed on Courtney's lips as she held the image of Luke in her mind. Then she turned and offered to fix Kevin a bowl of sliced peaches and cream.

"Yum," Kevin said.

"Actually, we'll put milk on them, because we don't have any cream, but they'll still taste good."

"Mom, do you like Luke?"

"Well, yes, of course I do."

"Do you like him a lot?"

"How much is a lot?"

"Well, enough to kiss him?"

"Kevin Marshall, since when do you think about things like kissing?"

"I wouldn't kiss no girl. The girls at my school are gross. Big people kiss, though, when they like each other a lot. Would you kiss Luke?"

"Let's go have some peaches," Courtney said, feeling the warm flush on her cheeks.

"Would you?" Kevin asked, following her into the kitchen. "Kiss Luke?"

"Kevin, why are you asking me these questions?"

He knelt on a chair, plunked his elbows on the table, and cupped his chin in his hands.

" 'Cause I like Luke, Mom, and so does Jessica. I was just thinkin' that if you like him enough to kiss him, and then Luke kissed you, then maybe he could be our dad."

"Oh, honey."

"I sure would like to have a dad," Kevin said in a small voice. "A neato dad, just like Luke. Would you try, Mom? Would you try to like Luke enough to kiss him so he could be our dad?"

"'Kevin . . .'" Courtney was unable to stop the tears that spilled onto her cheeks. She picked up Kevin, then sat back down in the chair with him on her lap. She held him tightly, rocking him back and forth as she'd done when he was a baby. "I love you, Kevin," she said, swallowing the lump in her throat.

"I love you, too, Mom. I know you have two scoops of love in your heart for me and Jessica, but . . ."

"I know, sweetheart, I know. It's not quite the same as having a daddy, is it? Oh, Kevin, I wish it were different, I really do."

"You could try, Mom. Luke is neato, he is! Will you think about kissing him? Please?"

"Honey, it's much more complicated than that."

"Please? Just think about it? Don't say no, okay? Please, Mom?"

"Yes, yes, all right. You're tired, and you're getting upset. Let's have our peaches; then I'll tuck you into bed."

"You won't tell nobody that I sat on your lap, will ya?"

"No, it will be our secret," she said, and kissed him on the top of his head.

" 'Kay. Mom?"

"Yes?"

"You're not mad 'cause I want a dad are you?"

"No, my darling, not at all. I understand, Kevin. With all my heart I understand."

"You're the bestis mom in the whole wide world, and Luke is— "

"Yes, I know, he's neato." She set Kevin on his feet. "Now! It's time for some peaches." Oh, poor Kevin, she thought. He sounded so wistful, so sad, when he talked about wanting a father, having neato Luke as his dad. Was it wrong to go out with Luke on Friday, to run the risk of Kevin's getting his hopes up? Was she being selfish by having a few stolen hours with Luke, without considering the effect it might have on her son? What a jumbled mess her life had become.

The peaches were consumed, Kevin was tucked into bed, and then Courtney typed on her computer until midnight. To her dismay, Luke's image now filled the small office along with the memory of the kisses they had shared. Luke was everywhere, it seemed, and Courtney moaned when he followed her up the stairs, then into her dreams.

At two A.M. Luke swore, threw back the blankets on his bed, and swung his feet to the floor. He rested his elbows on his knees and made a steeple of his fingers as he stared at nothing in the dark room.

Courtney, he fumed. There she was every damn minute, bugging the hell out of him. Why wouldn't she stay in her own house, where she belonged? She'd followed him home and now was in this bed, making him ache with wanting her.

At least he'd gotten things back on the track this evening. She had accepted his apology, then agreed to practice dating, with him in charge. That would fry ol' Leonard's bacon. Let him stew in his juice for a while. Actually, Leonard wasn't so bad. Not good enough for Courtney, of course, but fairly decent, considering he was a no-neck jock.

Luke sank back onto the pillow and laced his fingers under his head.

Was his aching desire for Courtney psychological? he wondered. Did he want her because he couldn't have her? No. Nice try, but no. His desire for her was real. And also real were all the glaring reasons why it wasn't going to happen. Oh, hell, why did she insist on having a husband, a father for those kids? Affairs were neat and tidy, unencumbered. They started and ended by mutual consent. Well, most of the time, anyway. But it was all or nothing for Courtney Marshall. Wedded bliss or forget it, Charlie. And for Courtney that was exactly how it should be.

Well, once he'd led her through the basics of dating, the dos and don'ts, she could find herself a hearth-and-home type. Maybe she *should* check out the PTA meetings. But not now, not yet. She wasn't ready. *He'd* decide when she'd graduated to the big league, because he was the coach.

Why in the hell was he doing this?

There it was again, Luke thought irritably, the bottom-line question. Why in the hell was he doing this? Because . . . because he was, that was all. Because he was basically a nice person, and Courtney needed his help. Just a humanitarian act on his part. And if Larry knew about it, he'd have Luke committed to the funny farm. Larry and Marsha had kept smiling those sick, know-it-all smiles at him all day today, but they had it pegged wrong. They figured he was hung up on a woman with two kids, which simply wasn't true. Hell, he was preparing her to go out and snag a husband. Another man. Someone else. Not him. A shadowy figure, with or without a neck, who would take Courtney into their wedding bed and . . .

"Dammit," Luke muttered. He rolled over onto his stomach and punched his pillow. Then, for lack of anything better to do, he punched it again.

After Kevin got home from school the next day, Courtney loaded both children into the car and drove to a large shopping mall to purchase new sneakers for Kevin and a larger supply of big-girl panties for Jessica. They visited the pet shop, which was an ongoing ritual, and ooh'd and aah'd over the puppies and kittens. Courtney was considering getting a dog, but would settle for one listed in the "For Free" column in the newspaper. As she bent over to peer at a basset hound, Jessica yelled from her stroller, "Lu, Lu."

"That's not too complimentary," Courtney said, laughing, as she stared at the wrinkled animal. "Do you really think that dog looks like Luke?"

"Lu!"

Courtney turned to see a tall blond man leaving the store with two children.

"That's not Luke, Jessica," Kevin said. "That's somebody else's dad."

Courtney looked quickly at Kevin, but he watched the man and children until they disappeared from view. Darn it, she thought, Kevin just didn't understand. In his beautiful little-boy world he was convinced that if she would only kiss Luke, everything would fall perfectly into place. He didn't realize how complicated being a grown-up was, how intricate the ways of love. It was glorious when it was right, and shattering when it was wrong. And Luke was wrong. She knew it, knew she mustn't fall in love with him, but didn't have the strength yet to tell Kevin it was hopeless, that Luke was not going to be his and Jessica's daddy. But she would tell him. Soon.

Courtney treated the children to hamburgers at a crowded fast-food restaurant. The trio was late getting home, and both junior members were bathed in record time and tucked into bed. Courtney had just entered her office to work when the telephone on the desk rang.

"Hello?" she said into the receiver.

"It's Luke. I've been worried about you. Where have you been? Are you all right? Are the kids okay? Why aren't you answering any of my questions?"

Courtney laughed. "Hello, Luke," she said, knowing her smile was firmly in place. "At the mall. Yes. And yes. How's that?"

"You were at the mall, and everyone is fine?"

"Right."

"Good. I just called to make sure you could get a sitter for Friday night."

"Yes, I'm all set."

"Should I pick her up?"

"No, she only lives two houses down. The kids like her. She has stayed with the children when I've had committee meetings or gone to the movies with a friend. She's a senior in high school."

"That young? I don't know, Courtney, maybe it would be better to hire a pro from an agency. Young girls talk on the phone all the time. What if she doesn't keep a close eye on Jessica and Kevin? They're fast on their feet. Yeah, let's get a licensed nurse, or whatever they have at those agencies."

"Don't be silly. Debbie is very responsible. She eats a lot, but she's still responsible."

"Well, okay, if you're sure. Are you sure?"

Courtney's smile grew even bigger. "I'm sure. I had no idea you were a worry wart."

"I'm not. Well, just a little, maybe. I've never had any dealings with kids before. It's disconcerting to be making decisions regarding their lives."

"Well, Debbie will take very good care of them. You know I wouldn't let anything happen to Jessica and Kevin."

"It's got to be rough, Courtney, being a single parent. The whole idea of it is starting to blow my mind. You never get any time off. You can't turn to someone and say, 'Hey, you decide if they should do this or that, because I'm all worn out.' Even if you have two scoops of love in your heart, enough for two parents, it's still a tough road to go."

"Sometimes," Courtney said. "But the rewards, despite those fleeting moments of mental and physical exhaustion, make it worth the trip down that road. A lot of the decisions are instinctive. I just know what's right or wrong for my children. It's hard to explain. I often understand them better than I do myself."

"I doubt that. You're one of those rare individuals who knows exactly who she is, and what she needs and wants."

"So are you."

"Me? Oh, well, yeah, I guess I am."

"Or, to be more precise, you know what you don't want," she said quietly.

"What?"

"Never mind. We're getting off on a psychological tangent here. How was your day?"

They talked for nearly an hour, going from one topic to the next in easy, comfortable conversation.

"Well, I'd better let you go," Luke said finally.

"Yes, I have typing to do yet tonight."

"Don't work too late."

"I won't. I'm very pleased with how it's going. I'm putting in eight or nine hours a day on the computer by dividing it up in segments around the kids' schedules. That's a full-time job, with no day-care costs, wardrobe worries, transportation."

"Am I paying you enough to do the typing for L and L?"

"I'm charging you an exorbitant fee, Mr. Hell and Hell, and you're paying it."

"Good for you. If my checks bounce, sue the pants off me."

"I intend to."

"So go type, lovely lady. I'll see you Friday night."

"Yes, all right. Good night, Luke," she said softly.

"Good night, Courtney. And, Courtney?"

"Yes?"

"It was really nice chatting with you like this. I've never done anything like it before. Well, see ya. 'Bye."

"Good-bye." She was smiling as she hung up the phone. Oh, Lu, Lu, Lu, she thought. There was a depth of caring within him that he wasn't even aware of. His concern about the baby-sitter was dear, and he was beginning to see what she faced as a single parent on a daily basis. Luke Hamilton was more, much more, than just an extremely handsome man. He was everything she could possibly hope to find in a husband, in a father for her children.

Were the tempestuous and confusing emotions within her actually love? she wondered. Was she falling in love with Luke? Did she want to look deep within herself to discover the answer? She didn't know. If only he would . . . No, she wasn't going to do that. She'd done the "if only" routine after Joe had died, but it hadn't changed the fact that he was gone.

But somehow this was different, Courtney realized. Luke was alive, was in her life, talking, laughing, sharing. Her feelings for him were growing. What would happen if she fell in love with him? No, facts were facts, and she had to face them. Luke didn't want the world she offered. Kissing him would not transform him into the children's father, as Kevin so adamantly stated. Luke was a free spirit and intended to stay one.

With a sigh she turned to her computer. She welcomed Luke's image as it swirled through her mind, and welcomed the tingle of desire within her. For now, for a little while, she'd just take one day at a time.

When Luke replaced the receiver he didn't release his hold on it, but instead stared at the telephone, frowning. He shifted his gaze to sweep slowly over the large living room, taking in the expensive furniture, the thick carpet.

There had never been toys on the floor, he realized. There had never been fingerprints on the tables or walls, or the sound of children's laughter filling the rooms. The time Kevin had come with him when he'd had to shower and change before baby-sitting, Kevin had been the first little boy to enter his house. House? Or home? House. Just a place were he slept, ate, brought women. It was a building without the inviting warmth that Courtney created in her less-than-fancy dwelling.

A chill swept through Luke, and the silence in the room beat against his temples. He pushed himself to his feet and crossed to the small bar on the far side of the room. He felt restless, bursting with a sudden surge of strange energy, and poured himself a stiff drink.

He could go work out at the gym, he supposed. It was open all night. No, he wasn't in the mood. Take a run on the beach, relax in the hot tub, mess around on the computer? No, none of those activities held any appeal. Find a bar with a band and listen to music, see who was out and on the loose? There were always women on the loose who . . .

"No," he said, then took a large swallow of the liquor. What had Courtney said? He knew what he *didn't* want. It seemed to him that that was just another way of saying he knew what he wanted. And he did know. He had everything he wanted. His life was set up exactly as he'd planned it. But he wasn't so hard-nosed that he wasn't flexible. After all, look at the screwball situation he was in with Courtney Marshall.

But that would be over soon, and he'd go back to living his own life.

"Ah, yes. Life in the fast lane," he said, scowling. He drained the glass, then poured himself another double. "Wine, women, and song. And silence." He wasn't in the mood for that silence. Hell, he wasn't in the mood for anything. Except . . . "Courtney," he mumbled. He finished the drink and poured another. "Seeing, kissing, touching, tasting Courtney."

He hiccuped.

"Here's to Courtney," he said, his words slightly slurred. He lifted his glass, then half-emptied it in one swallow. He splashed more liquor into the glass, and held it high in the air. "And here's to Jessica and Kevin, the cute little buggers."

Again he topped his drink, now staring moodily into the amber liquid.

"Lucky little buggers, too," he said, his words running together. "They're in a house that's a home, and Courtney loves 'em. Yeah, Courtney sure does love those kids. Those lucky, lucky kids. And they're nice kids, neat kids, A-OK. I like those kids. And I sure do like Courtney Marshall. Sure do. A helluva lot."

He tossed off the drink, squinted at the sofa across the room, then weaved his way forward. He reached the sofa just in time to pass out cold on the cushions.

At five o'clock the next afternoon Courtney was in the front yard with both children, supervising Kevin's watering of the grass that was growing to replace the golden meadows of poppies. Jessica was pushing a toy buggy around the yard, jabbering to the doll lying face down inside it.

"Jessica's in my way, Mom," Kevin said.

"No, she's not," Courtney said. "Don't even think about spraying her with that hose, Kevin. I mean it. I see the gleam in your eye."

"The what?"

"Don't spray her."

" 'Kay," he said with a sigh. "But she is in my way."

"I'm watching her. She's—" Courtney stopped speaking as she heard the low rumble of a powerful car engine. A moment later Luke's sports car came into view. He parked in front of the house. "Luke," she whispered.

"Luke!" Kevin yelled.

"Lu, Lu, Lu," Jessica said, running toward him.

It all happened so fast that Courtney couldn't seem to move. Luke stepped out of the car and swung Jessica up into his arms. An excited Kevin turned, hose in hand, and in the next instant sprayed Jessica and Luke with the cold water. Jessica shrieked. Luke swore. Kevin stared at them with wide eyes.

"Courtney!" Luke bellowed.

"Oh, good heavens," she said, snapping out of her trance. She grabbed the hose from Kevin and turned the nozzle to cut off the water.

Jessica wailed at full volume.

Kevin burst into tears.

Luke cut loose with a string of expletives.

"Don't you swear like that in front of my innocent children, Luke Hamilton," Courtney said, none too quietly.

"Innocent? Innocent! He nearly drowned me, and I'm freezing to death."

Kevin's wailing matched the volume of Jessica's.

"Now look what you've done," Courtney said.

"Me?" Luke roared.

"Give her to me." She snatched a soggy Jessica from Luke's arms. "Kevin, honey, it's all right. It was an accident. Some people"—she shot Luke a stormy glance—"are simply overreacting."

"Ha!" Luke said. "You're not standing here freezing your buns off."

"Would you watch your mouth?" Courtney asked. "You sound like a drunken sailor."

"Close," he muttered. "Very close."

"Let's all calm down and go into the house," Courtney suggested. "Come along, all of you. Jessica, hush, that's enough. Kevin, stop crying. It wasn't your fault. Luke, quit looking at my son as though you're going to murder him. You're scaring him to death."

"Mmm," Luke said, still frowning.

When the motley crew stood in the living room, water dripped onto the carpet.

"Okay, let's see here," Courtney said. "Kevin, you're dry except for your feet. Go put on your slippers."

" 'Kay," he said, running for the stairs. "Sorry, Luke," he called over his shoulder.

"It's okay, Kevin," Luke said. "I'm sorry I yelled. Forget you heard those words I said, too."

" 'Kay," Kevin said, smiling, then ran up the stairs.

"Now, then," Courtney said, "I'll give Jessica a bath, all I need is dry clothes, and—"

"And me?" Luke asked, grinning at her. "What are we going to do about me, sergeant? I'm ready to follow your orders, ma'am."

"Oh. Well. Oh."

"Yes?" Luke was all innocence as he leaned slightly toward her.

She glared at him again. "You," she said, "are to march your frozen buns up to my bathroom and take a hot shower."

"Tsk, tsk, such language," he said, starting toward the stairs. "One hot shower. Got it. Then what?"

"I'll put your clothes in the dryer."

"I swear, Courtney, you're just so organized and efficient. There's just one small problem."

"Which is?"

"What am I going to wear while my clothes are drying?" he asked, turning to look at her.

"Wrap up in a blanket, I guess."

"Yes, ma'am," he saluted sharply. "I shall return in a flash wrapped in a blanket, and stripped down to my bare bottom beneath it. Anything else, ma'am?"

"Go!"

He laughed, then took the stairs two at a time.

"I don't think I can handle this, Jessica," Courtney said.

"Lu," Jessica said, clapping her hands. "Lu, Lu, Lu."

Six

Courtney bathed Jessica in the bathroom at the end of the hall upstairs, then zipped the little girl into fuzzy pajamas with feet. The door to Courtney's bedroom was closed, and she could hear the sound of water running in the shower.

Do not think, she told herself as she carried Jessica back downstairs. Do not think about Luke in the shower. Her shower. Naked in her shower. Bronzed and magnificent and nude. Oh, good Lord.

"Okay," she said when she reached the living room. Kevin was sitting on the couch, watching television. "Slippers, Kevin? Good. You two watch 'Mr. Rogers' while I change my clothes. Then we'll eat."

" 'Kay," they said in unison.

Courtney went up the stairs, down the hall, then stopped outside her bedroom door.

Cute, she thought. She was cold and clammy, and couldn't go into her own room for dry clothes. What a ridiculous situation. Maybe she should have sent Luke home, drenched to the skin or not. No, it had been her son who had caused this fiasco, so it was up to her to fix it.

She knocked lightly on the door.

"Who's calling, please?" came a singsong response.

"May I come in?" Courtney asked, frowning.

"You bet, darlin'."

"Wrong question," she muttered. "Are you decent?" she said louder.

"Oh, at least. In fact, I've been told I'm pretty damn good."

"You're terrible, that's what you are," she said, bursting into laughter. "Darn it, Luke, I'm cold and wet."

The door was flung open, and a tanned hand grabbed her arm and hauled her into the room. Luke closed the door, then backed her against it, his hands braced on either side of her head. A blue blanket was tucked around his waist, he smelled like soap, and Courtney's knees went weak as she stared up at him.

"I'll warm you up," he said, his voice low. "Your lips look cold. Are your lips cold, Courtney?" He lowered his head toward hers. "Do you want my heat, Courtney Marshall?"

"Yes. Oh, yes," she said, hardly breathing.

He held his body away from her. As his mouth covered hers, they were the only parts of their bodies that were touching. But it was a kiss so sensuous that a moan purred from Courtney's throat. She slid her hands up Luke's bare chest, twining her fingers through the moist curly hair. He trembled as her palms skimmed over his flat nipples, and he inched closer. She slid her arms around his neck and urged him nearer, his chest brushing against her blouse.

"Cold and wet," he murmured, his lips still close to hers. With one hand he unbuttoned her blouse and brushed it aside. "Lovely," he said, his voice raspy, as he gazed at her full breasts pushing above her lacy bra. "I won't hurt you, Courtney. I just want to see you, touch you."

"Yes," she whispered.

He slipped the wet blouse from her shoulders and dropped it to the floor. Her bra followed an instant later. He filled his hands with the cool, soft flesh of her breasts, and a pulse beat wildly in his neck.

"Beautiful. So beautiful," he said, then dipped his head to draw one bud into his mouth. He suckled gently, rhythmically, his thumb moving with the same motion over the nipple of her other breast.

Courtney closed her eyes to savor the sweet pain rocketing through her. The trembling in her knees swept along her entire body, causing her to clutch Luke's shoulders for support. She felt as though she were floating away to a glorious place, a place with Luke. A pulsing heat deep within her matched the pull of his mouth on her breast. It was ecstasy. She was alive, every inch of her tingling and aware, wanting, needing more of what he was offering. A soft moan of pleasure escaped from her throat.

Luke brought his lips back to hers to capture the last of that breathy sound in his mouth and match it with a groan of his own. He slid his hand to her back, crushing her against him, molding her body to his as his tongue plummeted deep into her mouth.

Her hands slid up to the back of his head, her fingers into his thick hair, pressing his mouth harder to hers. Their breathing was labored, their hearts

thudd...
could f...
desire, ...

And sh...
suality, w...
she'd nev...
awakening...
dark cocoor...
ity and rejoi...

Luke's har...
breasts, nestl...
arched her bac...

"Courtney," h...
"Oh, Courtney, ...want you. Lord, ...ood. I
want you. Lord, ...

"Yes," she whis... want you. I do, Luke.
I do."

He slowly lifted his head to meet her gaze. Their
eyes were smoky with desire. With trembling hands
he cradled her face and backed away from her.

"I promised I wouldn't hurt you," he said hoarsely,
"and I won't. Don't be sorry about this, Courtney.
Please don't."

"No, no, of course I'm not sorry. I want you, Luke.
I want you to make love with me."

Luke stared at the ceiling for a long moment as he
strove for control. Then he dropped his hands and
stepped back.

"No," he said. "No, I can't."

Tears sprang to Courtney's eyes, and she wrapped
her arms over her breasts, suddenly aware of her
nakedness. She stared at the floor, unable to trust
her trembling legs to carry her across the room to
seek refuge in the bathroom. She was filled with the

ache of thwarted desire and the...
rejection, look at me,...
"Courtney," he...
She shook her head...
"please."
She slowly lift...
were tears c...
Not carin...
"Oh...

cold pain of Luke's

he murmured.

ed her gaze to his, knowing there
nging to her lashes, but not caring.
about anything.
Lord," Luke said, raking a hand through his
. "What have I done? Please don't cry. I'll get
dressed and leave. I'll never come near you again.
You can forget you ever met me, okay? Do you want
to hit me, or something? Would that help, make you
feel better? Do whatever it takes, but don't cry."

"Why?" she whispered.

"Why what?" he asked, confused.

"Why don't you want to make love with me? Why
did you kiss and touch me like that, then turn
away, reject me? Why, Luke?"

His hands shot out and gripped her shoulders
tightly as a muscle jumped along his jaw.

"Reject you! Lady, I nearly took you right here on
the floor. Stepping away from you was the most
difficult thing I've ever done in my life. I ache with
wanting you. I've imagined our lovemaking over and
over in my mind until I've nearly gone crazy. Whatever I do, wherever I go, you're there, filling my
thoughts. Not want you? I've never wanted anyone
the way I want you."

"Then why didn't you make love with me?" she
asked, her voice rising as tears spilled onto her
cheeks. "Here, on the floor, on the bed, wherever.
Why didn't you take what I was offering to you?"

"Because I care about you too damn much! Because the emotional hold you have on me is like

nothing I've ever experienced before." His grip on her tightened even more. "Because you scare the hell out of me, Courtney Marshall, that's why. I'm supposed to be preparing you to go out and find yourself a husband. Well, guess what? The thought of another man touching you is like a knife twisting in my gut. So help me, Courtney, I'd sure as hell better not find out I've fallen in love with you!"

Courtney blinked once, twice, then smiled. It was a gentle smile, a warm, soft, womanly smile.

"Oh," she said.

Luke dropped his hands from her shoulders and eyed her warily.

"Oh?" he repeated. "What's that supposed to mean?"

"That now I understand why you didn't make love with me." She picked up her blouse and bra and clutched them to her breasts as she looked at him again. "Would you mind checking on Jessica and Kevin while I change? I'll be down in a few minutes. Do you want to send out for pizza?"

"Pizza? Now we're talking about pizza?"

"To have for dinner while your clothes are drying. Would you call in an order and have it delivered?"

"Sure, but . . . Courtney, a few minutes ago you were crying, and now we're discussing pizza? This is nuts. You're really making me nervous. Are you in some kind of hysterical shock, or something?"

"Don't be silly. I asked you why you didn't make love with me, you explained it, and now it's time to think about dinner. Would you check on the kids?"

"Yeah, I'm going," he said, frowning at her.

"Thank you," she said, starting toward the bathroom. "I won't be long."

"Right." He ran a hand over the back of his neck.

"Weird," he muttered, then left the room, closing the door behind him.

"I love you," Courtney whispered. "I love you, Luke." She was in love with Luke Hamilton. And, as only love could be, it was beautiful, wondrous, creating a warm glow of happiness within her.

And maybe, just maybe, Luke loved her. There was a glimmer of hope, a fragile thread of a chance that he loved her. He was confused and angry about what he was feeling for her, had admitted his fear that his emotions might be out of control.

"One day at a time, Courtney," she said. "Take one day at a time."

As she dressed, her smile faded. Was she being fair? she wondered. Did Luke have the right to know that she'd canceled her husband hunt? But what could she tell him? That her plan was off because she'd fallen madly in love with him, and was waiting, hoping, praying, that his feelings for her would continue to grow? Considering his angry outburst over his mental dilemma, that didn't sound like a very good idea. What should she do? There were Kevin and Jessica to think of, too, and their increasing attachment to Luke. She wasn't just a woman in love, she was also a mother, and her children's emotional well-being was her responsibility. Oh, darn it, she really didn't know what to do.

"Well, pooh," she said, and marched from the room, the bundle of wet clothes in her arms.

Downstairs Luke was standing by the open front door, and a moment later Kevin ran in from outside.

"What's going on?" Courtney asked.

"I sent Kevin out to my car," Luke said, glancing at her over his shoulder. "Didn't want to get your neighbors all shook up traipsing around in my blanket. I brought some typing for you and computer games for Kevin."

"Neato," Kevin said.

"And thank you," Courtney said.

"Thanks, Luke," Kevin said. "Can we try one now?"

"Okay if we use the computer?" Luke asked Courtney. "I ordered the pizza."

"Yes, of course," she said.

"Come on, Jessica," Luke said. "There are great color graphics on these programs, Courtney. I want to see how long they hold Jessica's attention."

"Fine." Courtney watched as the trio disappeared into her office. "I like color graphics," she said in a small voice. Wonderful. She was pouting again.

In the laundry room off the kitchen she put the clothes in the dryer, then set out paper plates and napkins on the kitchen table, and sat down.

She relived in her mind the feel of Luke's hands and mouth on her breasts, and a wave of desire swept through her. She closed her eyes to savor each tantalizing memory, and a flush of arousal warmed her cheeks.

"Sleeping?"

Her eyes popped open. Luke was sitting across the table from her. She averted her gaze from his bare chest and stared at his chin.

"No, just thinking," she said.

"About?"

"Things."

"Like what happened between us in your bedroom?"

She met his gaze, but the expression on his face gave her no clue about his present mood.

"Yes," she said, looking at him steadily. "As a

matter of fact, that's exactly what I was thinking about."

"And?"

"And I'm not sorry it took place. Are you?"

"I'm not sure," he said, sighing. "I don't know. It was fantastic to touch . . . I'll skip the details. Yes, it was fantastic, but it only emphasized to me how much I want you and how scrambled my brain is right now. I care about you, Courtney. Hell, it goes deeper than just caring."

"Do you think . . . think maybe you're falling in love with me, Luke?" she asked softly.

"I have no idea what all these emotions mean. They're entirely foreign to me. But don't you see? Even if I did fall in love with you, all I would want is an affair. You need more than that. The truth is, if I *am* in love with you I don't want to know. What would be the point? I'm still the wrong man for you. You need a husband, a father for—"

"I canceled the husband hunt," she interrupted him.

"What?"

"You heard me."

"You canceled it? Why?"

"Why?" Oh, heavens, what was she going to say? She was a lousy liar, but if she told him that she loved him . . . Oh, help. "Because," she said, smiling brightly. "Because I did."

"Why?" he repeated, leaning forward and resting his arms on the table. "That's a simple question. Give me a simple answer."

"I've changed my mind? That's it." She smacked the table with her hand. "I've changed my mind."

"Why?"

"Darn it, Luke, you sound like a broken record.

Women do change their minds about things, you know."

"We're not talking about the color of your finger-nail polish here. We're discussing your husband."

"I don't want one," she said, deciding to examine the nails he'd just mentioned, only to discover she wasn't wearing any polish. "Nope. I've got enough to do without having to pick up some guy's dirty socks."

"Oh, yeah?" Luke said, scowling.

"Yep. When do you think the pizza will get here? I'm hungry."

"When did you make this momentous decision?"

"About being hungry?"

"Dammit, Courtney, knock it off. Quit playing around and tell me what's going on in your head. I'm your coach, remember? I have the right to know if I'm out of a job."

"Oh, well, you've got a point there. You're fired. I've decided to—to have an affair." What? What!

"What!" Luke yelled.

"Discreetly, of course." Oh, Lord, what was she saying? "There will be no hanky-panky in front of my children. Nothing . . . intimate will take place under this roof. Yes, an affair is just the ticket." Where was this bunch of bull coming from? she wondered. When she started lying she really got on a roll.

"I think you're lying through your teeth," Luke said, slouching back in the chair and crossing his arms over his chest.

"I certainly am not," she said, hoping she sounded thoroughly indignant. "I'm a woman of the eighties, and it's time I acted like one. I don't need a husband in order to be complete. I'm doing just fine on my own, thank you. As I see it, an affair will do nicely. I can satisfy my natural biological urges, and I don't have to pick up some guy's dirty socks. Pretty smart, huh?"

Luke narrowed his eyes and stared at her intently, looking, Courtney thought frantically, as though he were peering right into her brain.

"Interesting," he said finally. "Very interesting."

"Sophisticated is the word."

"Oh, yes, by all means." His tone was dry. "An affair is sophistication to the max. Just when are you planning to launch your new campaign?"

"Soon."

"I see." He laced his fingers behind his head and stared at the ceiling. "Is Friday night soon enough?"

"What?"

"Well," he said slowly, looking at her again, "who am I to argue with you? If you've changed your mind about a husband, so be it. It seems to me that this solves a lot of our problems."

Her eyes widened. "It does?"

"Why, sure, darlin'." He smiled a dazzling smile. "We want each other, right? We physically desire each other. Now we're on the same wavelength about commitment, the forever-and-ever jazz. Whadda ya say, Courtney? Shall we do it? Have an affair?"

"I . . . um . . . The pizza person is knocking at the door."

"I'll go," he said, getting to his feet. "My treat. You can give me your answer after dinner."

"You betcha," Courtney said, then pressed her hand to her forehead as Luke left the room. Saints above, what had she done? She had been so afraid that Luke would make a beeline for the door if she told him that she loved him, but now look at the mess she'd gotten herself into. An affair? With Luke?

A temporary, here-today-gone-tomorrow fling? She wanted to spend the rest of her life with that man!

Luke reappeared with the pizza in his hands and Kevin and Jessica on his heels. Courtney hardly tasted the gooey, delicious food, and only commented absently when spoken to during the meal. When the buzzer sounded on the dryer, she jumped out of her chair and hurried to the laundry room. A minute later she shoved Luke's dry, warm clothes at him. He dressed upstairs, and when he returend to the kitchen Kevin asked if he could play on the computer some more. Courtney gave her permission, and Luke started toward her office with the two children.

"I won't be long," he said to Courtney before leaving the kitchen. She smiled weakly.

In Courtney's office Luke loaded a game disk into the computer, then gave Kevin instructions as to which keys would move the cartoon figures around the screen.

"A friend of mine wrote this program," he said. "You have to collect the alphabet in the bear's mouth in the correct order, or you can't get out of the cave to get that treasure chest."

"Neato," Kevin said.

"Neat. Toe," Jessica said, clapping her hands.

"You're doing fine," Luke said. "I'll come back and check on you in a bit."

" 'Kay," Kevin said.

All right, Luke thought, walking slowly out of the office, now to sort through this news flash of Courtney's. What in the hell was she up to? She was canceling the husband hunt to have an affair? Courtney? It didn't add up. Then again, he'd never claimed to be able to understand women's minds.

He'd flung out his Friday-night offer to gauge her reaction, but she'd been fairly cool. Dammit, was she actually serious about this?

So now what? he wondered. He was about to walk back into that kitchen and find out her answer about their affair. What if she said yes? Could he do it, engage in an affair with her knowing it was wrong for her? It would suit his needs perfectly, but what a rotten thing to do to her. Yet, if he bowed out of the picture, would she look further? Would she case the singles bars to find a candidate for her new campaign? He'd strangle her!

"Hell, what a mess," he muttered. "I'm aging before my very eyes."

He stopped in the kitchen doorway and leaned his shoulder against the frame, crossing his arms loosely over his chest. Courtney was pushing the chairs in at the table, and had a deep frown on her face. He cleared his throat. She jumped.

"Oh," she said, looking at him. "You're back."

"Yep."

"Would you like some ice cream?"

"No, thank you."

"Oh."

"You seem a little nervous, Courtney."

"Me? Nervous? Why would I be nervous?" she asked, wringing her hands.

He shrugged. "I don't know. Why would you be nervous? Unless, of course, you've thought through the plans for your new campaign and decided it wasn't a great idea. Don't let that upset you. I understand. Some people just aren't cut out to have affairs."

"I'm perfectly capable of having an affair, Luke Hamilton," she said, planting her hands on her hips.

"I'm a grown woman who knows her own mind, controls her own destiny. I fully intend to proceed with my new plans."

"Oh, yeah?"

"Yes," she said, tilting her nose in the air. "And as for Friday night, I . . . Well . . ."

"Yes?" he said, raising his eyebrows.

Oh, good Lord, Courtney thought, she was going to faint.

"Courtney?"

"I think you're absolutely right. We obviously feel a strong physical attraction for each other, so why not . . ." Her voice trailed off to a strange-sounding squeak. ". . . have an affair?"

"You're sure?"

"Oh, yes."

"Are you . . . prepared for this step?"

"Prepared?"

"I don't imagine you'd want to raise *three* children alone," he said, looking at her steadily. There, he thought smugly. That ought to scare her back to her senses.

"Oh. Good point. Well, no problem."

"What?" He pushed himself away from the doorjamb. "Why in the hell are you prepared? Ah-ha! Leonard. Before you went out with Leonard you—"

"I did not! How dare you insinuate such a thing. Not that it's any of your business, but I've been on the pill since Jessica was born, to correct some minor irregularities. Satisfied? Lord, you're nosy."

"Nosy? Hey, I'm the other half of this venture, remember? I have the right to know if I'm to be responsible for protecting you. It was an extremely reasonable question. But then, you wouldn't know that, would you, since you've never had an affair before."

"How tough can it be?" she said, shrugging.

"Oh, man," Luke said, shaking his head. "Okay, Ms. Worldly and Wise, you've got a deal. I'll pick you up Friday night at eight, we'll go out to dinner, then we'll go back to my place for a nightcap and . . . whatever."

"Whatever?" she repeated.

"Whatever, darlin'," he said, his voice low and rumbly. Then, as an afterthought, he winked at her. Courtney stopped breathing. "Well, I've got to shove off," he said. "I'll go say good night to the kids."

Courtney drew in a large gulp of air and braced her hand on the table for support. Whatever? she thought. Well, yes, of course she knew that. On Friday night she was going to make love with Luke Hamilton. She knew that. They'd go out to dinner, then to his house, take off their clothes, and . . . She knew that. Would her parents mind if she showed up on their doorstep in Florida tomorrow with two kids in tow?

"Shape up, Courtney," she said aloud. "Let's have a little sophistication here." But oh, mercy, how had she gotten herself into this? She'd opened her big mouth, that was how. But was having an affair with Luke really that bad an idea? The alternative was to tell him that she loved him, then watch his gorgeous backside exiting stage left. Something was better than nothing, and an affair was the only thing being offered. There was still the question of the children's attachment to Luke to be considered, and she'd have to listen carefully to the things Kevin said. But in the meantime she was going to do it. She'd have an affair with Luke.

She nodded decisively and walked into the living room. Luke was coming out of the office, and they met at the front door.

"See ya," he said.

"Thank you for the pizza."

"Sure. Oh, just call Marsha whenever you're finished with that typing, and she'll swing by and pick it up."

"Fine."

"Well, good night."

"Good night, Luke."

"Courtney, look, I don't think . . . Forget it." He yanked the door open. "I'll be here Friday night. 'Bye."

" 'Bye," she said softly, and the door closed behind him.

Luke didn't realize he was clenching his jaw so tightly until his teeth began to ache. He stopped at a red light and drummed his fingers impatiently on the steering wheel.

He was mad as hell at Courtney Marshall, he decided, pressing on the gas pedal as the light turned green. Anger. Yes, that was what he was feeling. And guilt for having agreed to have an affair with her. And anticipation at the thought of making love with her. And fear. Fear that once he'd taken that step, he'd be lost, unable to walk away from her.

Because he loved her.

He was in love with Courtney, and he might as well face that fact head on. He loved her . . . and now what? Lord, he was confused. If he hightailed it out of her life, she'd probably call No-neck Leonard in to take his place on the affair docket. No way.

He drove toward his house, but the thought of the large, silent rooms was unappealing. On impulse he turned in the opposite direction and drove to Anne and Larry's. The lights were on in the beach-front home, but Anne's car wasn't next to Larry's. Luke swung out of his sports car and strode to the door. Larry answered his insistent knock.

"Luke," Larry said, "leave the door on the hinges, will ya?"

"Sorry," Luke said, stepping into the living room. "Am I disturbing something?"

"Nope, I'm all alone. Anne is the guest speaker at a women's group tonight. I was sitting out on the deck. Want a beer?"

"Scotch."

"Uh-oh," Larry said. "Scotch plus the frown on your face says you've got troubles. Go out on the deck. I'll bring you a stiff drink."

Luke did as he was instructed, but rather than sit on one of the comfortable, padded lounge chairs, he paced back and forth across the deck. Larry delivered the promised drink, then sat down to watch Luke steadily trek back and forth. The minutes ticked by. Larry waited.

"I can't believe this," Luke muttered, not halting his pacing. Larry kept silent. "I can't pretend it isn't true, but I still can't believe it. Why me? I had my life all mapped out exactly how I wanted it, and now this. Hey, she's great, really special, but . . . And two kids? Well, yeah, they're fantastic kids, but . . . I'm not cut out for this. You can understand that, can't you, Larry? You and I think alike. No, we don't, not anymore. You're a married man. Some best friend you are. It seems to me that if a man doesn't want to be in love, he should be able to just turn it off, ignore it, or something. Right? Right."

"Wrong," Larry said.

"I was afraid of that," Luke said, slouching into a chair. He took a large swallow of his drink.

"Courtney Marshall?" Larry asked.

"Courtney Marshall," Luke said miserably.

"She's really something, huh?"

"Like no one I've ever met before, Larry. She's open, honest, so damn beautiful, and her life centers on her family. She could make a guy feel like a million bucks when all he did was walk in the door."

"That's nice," Larry said, nodding. "And the kids?"

"Oh, hey, they are smart buggers, those kids. Cute, too. Jessica calls me Lu, but I'm working on that. Kevin follows me around as if I'm a hero. I'm going to help him with his baseball. I took some computer games over there tonight. Do you know that Jessica recognizes red and blue when she sees them? She's only two. I yelled at Kevin because he drenched me with the hose, but he forgave me. That's class. The kid doesn't hold a grudge."

"When are you going to marry Courtney, Luke?" Larry asked quietly.

"As soon as I can convince her that I love her, and that I'd be a good husband and father," Luke said, then drained his glass.

"Good," Larry said. "I'm glad. You and I have been close friends for a long time, buddy, and I think it's time for this, it really is. Aren't you fed up with being lonely?"

"Lonely?" Luke repeated. "I didn't even know I was lonely until I met Courtney. Damn, I love her. And I love those kids. I want it, Larry, all of it, everything that Courtney has to offer. Can you believe this?"

"I can believe it. So? How tough a road do you have to go here? Does Courtney love you? How does she feel about marrying again?"

"I might be in pretty good shape if the husband hunt were still in effect, but now she's on an affair kick because of the dirty socks."

"What?"

"Aren't you listening to me?"

"That didn't make any sense. Dirty socks?"

"Oh, well, she suddenly decided she didn't want a husband after all. We agreed to have an affair."

"Tacky."

"Better me than Leonard."

"Who?"

"A no-neck jock who . . . Never mind. I need a program, a plan. She's all charged up about having an affair. If I bring up marriage now, I might find myself out on the sidewalk."

"This is getting complicated, Lucas."

"Tell me about it. I've got to give the impression that I'm all for the affair, then somehow show her that she's really not cut out for that stuff, and get her to reactivate the husband hunt. Then I move in for the kill. Get it?"

"Not really, but that's all right. Just one bit of advice from an old married man, here. Women are not stupid. Games have a way of backfiring, pal. Honest and up front works a helluva lot better."

"Maybe, but my circumstances are unique. I have to bide my time. Yeah, I'm getting a handle on this. Everything is under control."

"When dealing with a woman? Don't bank on it, Luke."

"No sweat. Hey, I feel better. I'm sure glad I came by here, Larry. I was scared to death when I realized I was in love with Courtney. Mad as hell, too. But now this whole thing is terrific. Luke Hamilton, husband and father. Pretty good, huh?"

"Yep," Larry said, smiling. "Damn good."

The two men fell silent, each lost in his own thoughts. The only sound in the star-studded night was the quiet lapping of the waves against the sandy shore.

"Larry," Luke said finally.

"Hmm?"

"It's going to be really, really great not being lonely."

Seven

On Friday night Courtney wore a simply-cut, teal blue crepe dress with a scooped neckline and gathered skirt. She looked, she decided as she draped a matching shawl around her shoulders, extremely sophisticated. Now, if she could just get the butterflies in her stomach to fly in some kind of sophisticated order, she'd be all set.

"You look beautiful," Luke said as he assisted her into his car.

"Thank you. So do you."

He chuckled as he slid behind the wheel. Courtney hadn't looked directly at him yet, he thought as he pulled away from the curb. She'd said hello to the knot of his tie, then busied herself kissing the children good-bye and telling Debbie, the baby-sitter, to help herself to the snacks. It was understandable that Courtney was nervous. Hell, *he* was nervous. But she had to relax, or the evening would be a disaster. He had to say something to get her to lighten up.

"Courtney?"

"What!" she yelled.

Luke jerked in surprise.

"Sorry," she said.

"Look . . . um, I think there's something you don't quite understand," he said, glancing quickly at her.

"Oh?"

"Just because we agreed to have an affair, doesn't automatically mean we're going to make love tonight," he said. It didn't? Lord, he was dying. No, patience was the key word here.

"It doesn't?" she asked.

"No. There's more to affairs than just sex."

"There is?"

"Well, sure." Like what? he asked himself. He had to think of something. "Conversation is nice. Talking about . . . stuff. All I'm saying is, if this isn't the right time for you to make love with me, then we won't. I want it to be special for both of us." Because he loved her, he added silently. "Okay?"

"Okay," she said, smiling. "Thank you for saying that. I guess I was more nervous than I realized. My lack of sophistication is certainly showing."

"You're perfect just the way you are, Courtney," he said quietly. "Don't try to be something you're not."

What she was, Courtney mused, was in love with Luke Hamilton. How handsome he was in his tan suit and light blue shirt and pastel patterned tie, his hair thick and golden, his skin bronzed, his shoulders so wide. And she *did* want to make love with him tonight. It was all the other nights of her life she was worried about, the ones without Luke, the lonely ones when their damnable affair was over.

Luke cared for her, was possibly even falling in love with her, she told herself yet again. She was holding fast to the thread of hope that he wouldn't leave her after all, that he would see the happiness he could reap from a life shared with her, Kevin, and Jessica. It was a thin, fragile thread, but it was all she had.

"Jessica is really smart for a two-year-old, don't you think?" Luke said.

"Yes, but I'm prejudiced. Tell me all about L and L. I have some idea of what you do from the typing, but I'm sure there's more. Marsha said you use a sophisticated computer system to keep everything running smoothly."

"Yes, we do. You know, when Kevin gets older he'll be a computer whiz. He has great coordination already. I've never had to repeat instructions, either. He listens, then gets it the first time. Smart, smart kid."

"Yes, he is. When did you start L and L?"

"I'm thinking about asking my friend to write a program especially for Jessica. I'll have him work out a game so she can learn the rest of the colors."

"Luke."

"I don't want to push her, but she's so bright. I'll check it all out with a child psychologist before I—"

"Luke."

"Yes?"

"This may sound rather strange, but I'd prefer not to talk about Jessica and Kevin tonight. It's not often that I get to be Courtney the woman instead of Courtney the mother. They don't need me thinking about them right now. They're safe with Debbie, having fun, eating junk food that I don't usually allow them to have. I'm the furthest thing from their minds, and that's fine. So I'm going to take these hours for myself, for us. All right?"

"Very all right," Luke said, smiling. "You are some kind of lady, Courtney Marshall. You really are. You're making me feel ten feet tall. There's the restaurant up ahead. How does Courtney the woman like the idea of sharing a bottle of their finest champagne?"

"Marvelous."

They were smiling as they entered the elegant restaurant, and they were smiling as they ordered their dinners and lifted their champagne glasses in a toast. They were smiling as they ate the delicious food and talked in low voices. They lingered over after-dinner coffee, and the smiles faded.

Their eyes met and their heartbeats quickened. Courtney saw only Luke as the room seemed to fade away. There was no sound of clinking china or muted voices. There was only Luke, and the echo of her pounding blood in her ears. His green eyes changed to a smoky hue, revealing his desire, for her. He reached for her hand, and his warmth spread throughout her. She remembered the feel of his hands and mouth on her breasts, and a flush crept into her cheeks. She couldn't move, and could hardly breathe, mesmerized by Luke's seductive gaze.

"Shall we go?" he asked, his voice husky.

"Yes," she whispered.

"To my place? For brandy?"

This was it, Courtney thought. Luke was giving her one last chance to change her mind. She wasn't a child. She knew what she was agreeing to if she went to his house. She could ask him to take her home. She was about to make a decision that would have a tremendous impact on the rest of her life.

Why was she so calm? she wondered. Where had

the butterflies zoomed off to? What was this strange combination of excitement and inner peace? It was love. Love for Luke.

"A brandy sounds perfect," she said, smiling at him. "I'm ready to go."

Luke signaled to the waiter for the check. His heart was thundering, and a trickle of sweat ran down his back.

Get it together, Hamilton, he told himself firmly as he draped Courtney's shawl around her shoulders. Every instinct he had was telling him to treat Courtney as reverently as if this were their wedding night. But if he did, he'd blow it. He had to show her that affairs weren't good enough for her, and then, at the right moment, offer her more. Offer? Beg might be closer to the mark. He wanted to spend the rest of his life with this woman. So much was at stake in the next few hours.

During the drive to Luke's, Courtney started three conversations, only to have Luke give brisk, one-syllable replies. She gave up, keeping silent as she peered at him from beneath her lashes. He was tense, she realized, seeing his tight hold on the steering wheel and the muscles twitching in his jaw. Luke Hamilton, playboy *extraordinaire*, was nervous? No, that was ridiculous. He made a career out of this type of evening, was a pro at seduction and affairs. Was he having second thoughts because she wasn't as experienced as the women he was accustomed to? Well, that was rude. He wanted experience? She'd show him experience!

Luke pulled into the driveway of his house and turned off the ignition. He didn't speak as he assisted Courtney from the car and, his hand lightly cupping her elbow, led her to the front door. In the living room he flicked a switch on the wall, bringing four lamps to life in the large room.

"Oh, my," Courtney said, walking slowly forward, "this is lovely, exquisite. Did you have it professionally decorated?"

"Yeah," he said. He shrugged out of his jacket and tugged off his tie. He tossed both on a chair, then undid two buttons on his shirt. After hesitating a moment, he undid two more buttons. "Brandy?"

"Yes, please. This room is just the perfect blend of masculinity and warmth. I'm very impressed."

"Thanks," he said, handing her a brandy snifter. "May I take your shawl?"

"Certainly." Oh, good Lord, she thought. There was his yummy chest just calling to her to run her fingers through that curly, tawny hair. Well, why not? Someone with lots of experience would, right? Absolutely.

Luke drew the shawl away from her, then bent his head to trail a ribbon of kisses across the soft skin of her neck and shoulders. But as his lips skimmed over her, her hand inched inside his open shirt, and he stiffened.

"Is something wrong?" she asked.

"What? Oh, no, of course not. I just didn't want to spill my brandy on your dress."

"Good thought," she said, undoing two more buttons on his shirt. "I wouldn't want to spill it on your shirt, either." She pulled it free of his pants, then leaned forward to place a feathery kiss on his warm skin.

Luke's eyes widened, and he felt as though he'd been punched in the stomach as desire tightened within him. He slid his hand through Courtney's silken curls, and when she lifted her head he brought his mouth down hard onto hers. He knew the kiss was too rough, but he continued to ravish her mouth, plunging his tongue deep within.

Stick to the plan, he told himself frantically. He had to make her see that she deserved better than this. Why was her hand on his chest again? Now it was sliding to his back. Her breasts. She was pressing those luscious breasts against him. She was killing him. He had to stay in control to execute his plan!

"Courtney," he said, his voice harsh with passion, "the brandy."

"Who? Oh, the brandy. Yes, of course. Are you going to show me your hot tub?"

"Good idea," he said, nodding. "Excellent, in fact. Come on. It's in my bedroom."

"It is?"

"Yep, it is." He peered at her over the rim of his snifter as he took a sip. "That's where it is, all right."

"I'm certainly eager to see it," she said, placing her snifter on the bar.

"You are?" he asked, plunking his snifter next to hers with a thud.

"Wouldn't miss it for the world," she said in a breathy voice.

He shrugged. "A hot tub is a hot tub. Seen one, you've seen them all."

"But I want to see yours," she said, walking her fingers up his chest.

Luke grasped her busy hand and started across the room.

"Fine," he said gruffly. "I'll give you the twenty-five-cent tour."

Courtney was nearly lifted off her feet as Luke

hauled her down a hall, then into a bedroom. He flicked a switch that sent a rosy glow over one corner of the enormous room, illuminating the hot tub. It was on a raised platform next to floor-to-ceiling windows that afforded a fantastic view of the millions of stars in the heavens. Courtney slipped her hand from Luke's and walked over to the bottom of the wraparound stairs.

"How does it work?" she said.

The plan, the plan, Luke reminded himself. This setup was made to order. He'd start kissing her; then, the next thing she knew, they'd be naked in that tub. Then he'd—oh, hell, he couldn't do it! That was cheap seduction, standard operating procedure for an affair or a quickie roll in the hay, and he couldn't do it to his Courtney, his love. He couldn't take what she might not be ready to give.

"Luke," Courtney said, bringing him from his jumbled thoughts, "how does this work?"

"What? Oh, like this." He walked across the room and flipped a switch on the wall. The water began to churn in the black marble tub.

"It looks inviting," Courtney said wistfully. "I can just imagine what those warm bubbles would feel like on my skin."

Luke stifled a moan and rolled his eyes. When he looked at Courtney again, there was a rushing noise in his ears.

"What are you doing?" he asked, his voice strained.

"You don't mind if I wiggle my toes in there, do you?" she said, dropping her panty hose onto the floor next to her shoes. "Now, let's see how I can do this without getting my dress wet. I could sit on the edge there, I guess, and pull my dress above my knees."

"Oh, Lord," Luke said, leaning back against the wall for support.

"No, with my luck I'd fall in and be a soggy mess. Well, there's only one solution. The dress has got to go."

"What?" His voice was a croak. "Courtney, wait just a damn minute."

"Why? What's wrong?" she asked as she pulled down the back zipper.

"Don't do that," he said, raising his hand.

"I have a teddy on underneath."

"Oh, Lord, a teddy." He ran his hand down his face. "Those are the sexiest . . . Would you please stop and think about what you're doing?"

"You know, Luke"—the dress inched lower—"I'm beginning to think"—and lower—"that you've changed your mind about our affair." The dress fell in a heap at her feet.

"Oh . . . my . . . Lord," Luke muttered as his smoldering gaze swept over her. The teddy was pale blue, cut high on the sides and low in the front. His blood ran hot in his veins and his manhood stirred as he drank in the sight of her. "So beautiful," he said, his voice sounding strange to his own ears.

"Did you, Luke?" she asked softly. "Did you change your mind? Don't you want me after all?"

"You don't understand."

"I want *you*, Luke. I want to make love with you. I want to feel the warm bubbles in the hot tub, and then I want to feel you inside me, loving me, giving, taking, sharing. But if you don't want—"

"That's it," he said with a growl, striding over to her and grabbing her by the upper arms.

The kiss was long and powerful as their tongues met and twined seductively. Their bodies were pressed close together and their hands roamed and caressed, explored and delighted, until Courtney thought she would collapse. Luke skimmed the teddy from her slender body, and his sharp gasp voiced his pleasure as his gaze swept over her nakedness. With slightly trembling hands he shed his own clothes, then watched the expression of wonder on Courtney's face.

"You are magnificent," she whispered.

"You're not frightened, are you, Courtney?" he asked, cradling her face in his hands. "I don't want to frighten you. It's so important to me that this be good for you, perfect. I'll stop right now if you're not sure."

She smiled warmly at him and slid her arms around his neck. She nestled against his hot body, and his arousal pressed against her, announcing his need and his promise. He kissed her deeply, then took her hand and led her into the hot tub.

"Oh, it's heavenly," she said as she sank into the swirling water.

Luke smiled and sat down beside her. He trailed his thumb along her jaw, then down the slender column of her neck to the wildly beating pulse at the base. They were going to make love, he thought. Together, as one, they'd share something incredible, special. He wanted to tell her that he loved her, but this wasn't the time. She thought they were just having an affair, nothing more, and might believe that his declaration was his standard fare for the occasion.

Her actions were speaking volumes. She was obviously a very willing participant in their affair. Damn, he'd messed it up, blown his plan, but he'd lost control. Now how in the hell was he going to convince her that she deserved better than this? Hell, the "this" was close to picture-perfect!

"Why are you frowning?" she asked.

"I didn't know I was."

"What were you thinking about?"

"Do you have any idea how beautiful you are, Courtney?"

"I can't answer a question like that," she said, laughing. "Do you have any idea how handsome you are?"

"Sure."

"Figures."

"I love it when you laugh," he said, leaning toward her.

"Then I'll try to laugh as often as I can."

He captured her mouth with his, then slid his hands to her waist and lifted her across his lap. His arm cradled her head as he caressed her breasts, which were glistening with droplets of water. He shifted her higher; then his mouth closed over a taut nipple and suckled with a rhythmic motion. His hand roamed lower to the flat plane of her stomach, then on to the pulsing heat between her thighs.

"Luke," she said, gasping.

"I won't hurt you," he murmured, seeking her mouth again. "Trust me, Courtney."

"I do. Yes, I trust you," she whispered. And she loved him.

Wondrous sensations swept through Courtney as Luke worked his tantalizing magic with hands and lips and teeth and tongue. She was awash with desire, and tiny whimpers escaped from her throat along with soft sighs of pleasure. A sweet aching deep within her threatened to consume her, and she clung to Luke's shoulders. He was giving her so much, so very much, and she could feel him trembling from the force of his restraint. She wanted to give in return, be woman to his man.

"Luke. Oh, Luke," she said, burying her face in his shoulder as spasms of ecstasy rippled through her.

"That's it," he said hoarsely. "I want to pleasure you, Courtney. I want to do this for you."

"But—"

"Shh. I'll have my turn. This is for you."

"Luke!"

He held her tightly as she writhed in ecstasy; then she went limp in his arms, her eyes tightly closed.

"Courtney?"

"Oh, Luke," she said, slowly lifting her lashes, "that was . . . You are . . . I am so . . ."

"That," he said, smiling at her, "is how you're supposed to be feeling."

"And you?" she asked, splaying her hand on his chest.

"In due time. You'd better rest a minute."

"No need," she said, and her hand dipped below the water.

"Courtney, my control is at its outer limit, so . . ."

"So?" Her hand slid lower. "I'm waiting for you, Luke."

"Are you insatiable, lady?"

"Don't know."

"Well, I—Courtney!"

In a smooth, powerful motion, he stood up with her in his arms and stepped out of the hot tub. He crossed to the bed and laid her down, towering above her.

"Come to me, Luke," she said, lifting her arms.

With a throaty groan he lowered his body onto

hers, then entered her with a thrust that took her breath away. She wrapped her arms around his back, relishing the feel of his warm skin and hard muscles. Harder, stronger, he moved within her, carrying her up and away, back to ecstasy. He followed the path of her journey, higher, higher, until only seconds apart they toppled over the edge into rapture.

"Courtney."

"Luke. Oh, my, Luke."

They lay motionless, arms and legs entangled. Finally Luke kissed her deeply and moved away, then wrapped his arm around her waist. She snuggled close to his side, placing her hand over his heart to feel its steady beating.

"Fantastic," he said, his lips resting lightly on her forehead.

"Yes. More than I have words to tell you. I guess . . ." Her voice trailed off.

"You guess what?"

"That we're physically compatible. That's important in an affair, I would imagine," she said quietly. Oh, dammit, she was so sick of the term *affair* and everything it represented.

"Yeah, it's important," Luke said, frowning. It was important in a marriage too. Well, Courtney was gung-ho about an affair now, but good. And why not? They'd just shared an incredibly beautiful experience, and she didn't have to pick up his dirty socks. Damn, what a complicated mess.

"Oh, I'm so sleepy and contented, but I've got to get home."

"That's an affair for you," he said, swinging his legs over the edge of the bed. "Someone has to get up and go home."

"Well, I didn't mean right this second." She struggled to sit up. "I thought snuggling together like that was very nice, special."

"Well, sure, darlin', but facts are facts," he said, pulling on a pair of jeans. "You've got two kids waiting for you at home. Oh, well, no one ever said that affairs were the greatest arrangement in the world." Not bad, he thought smugly. The conversation was taking a turn in his direction. Courtney needed to think about the other side of the coin a bit.

"You don't particularly like affairs?" she asked, beginning to get dressed. Oh, dear heaven, was he dusting her off? Working up to telling her it had been a one-night stand? She'd drown him in his hot tub!

He tugged a T-shirt on over his head. "They'll do in a pinch. I'll meet you in the living room," he added as he strode out the door on his long legs.

"Do in a pinch?" Courtney repeated. "That's the most insulting thing I've ever heard. Well, what do you expect when you're an affairee, or affairor, or whatever I am. Lord, I hate this." But she loved Luke Hamilton, she thought, sighing, so she was stuck in the damnable affair. But do in a pinch? Blah.

She was suddenly tired, and she wearily pushed her feet into her shoes and finger-combed her hair. She wanted to curl up into a ball next to Luke and sleep the night away. She wasn't cut out for this lifestyle, she decided dismally, but there was no other option open to her except losing Luke altogether. But how long could she handle this grim routine of making love, pulling her clothes back on, and going home? It was so unappealing. Part of loving a man was that surge of joy when you reached out in the night to touch him to feel his strength and warmth.

Yes, the lovemaking she had shared with Luke had been beyond description in its beauty and splendor. But she needed more. She needed commitment, marriage, the promise of tomorrows until death parted them. But all she could do was hang on for now, hoping that Luke would come to want all of those things too.

"Oh, dear," she said with a sigh, then left the bedroom.

Luke felt the familiar knot tighten in his stomach when Courtney entered the living room. He wanted to pull her into his arms and kiss away her sad expression. He'd been brisk and cool, strictly business as he'd gotten dressed, and it had been like a knife twisting in his gut. But he had to do it this way to convince Courtney that an affair was wrong for her, for them. Dammit, he wanted to marry her tomorrow. Today. Hell, yesterday.

"Ready?" he asked, forcing a lightness to his voice.

"Yes," she said, picking up her shawl.

"It was a wonderful evening, all of it," he said, his voice low.

"Yes, it was."

"But all good things, and all that jazz," he rushed on, reaching for the doorknob.

"Brother," Courtney said under her breath.

In the car she leaned her head back and closed her eyes. Luke glanced over at her and frowned, but kept silent as he drove away from the house. No words were spoken during the entire drive to Courtney's.

"Looks like a Christmas tree," Luke said as he parked in front of her house.

"What?" she said, lifting her head. "Goodness, every light in the house is on. Debbie has never done that before. Something must be wrong." She reached for the door handle. "I didn't leave a telephone number because I didn't know which restaurant . . . I've got to get in there."

"Okay," Luke said, opening his door, "but take it easy. Calm down."

Courtney was already running toward the house. Luke caught up with her just as she entered the living room.

"Debbie?" she called. "Debbie?"

"Hi," the young girl said, bouncing down the stairs. "Have fun?"

"Debbie, what's going on?" Courtney asked.

"Oh, I've got it all under control, Mrs. Marshall. I just helped my mom through this with my brother and sister. I've got the old washing machine chugging its little heart out and—"

"Debbie, what are you talking about?" Courtney asked, her voice rising.

"The flu," Debbie said, smiling. "Jessica and Kevin are tossing their cookies all over the place. This is great training for me, since I plan to be a nurse."

"Oh, good Lord," Courtney said.

"Go see to Jessica and Kevin," Luke said. "I'll pay Debbie and walk her home."

"Yes, all right, thank you," Courtney said, running toward the stairs. "I'm so sorry, Debbie."

"A little bucket brigade never hurt anybody," Debbie said with a shrug.

"I'll walk you home," Luke said.

"Great. I hope some of my friends drive by. I'll tell them that you are the new love of my life, and they'll be green. Absolutely green. About the shade of Jessica and Kevin at the moment."

"How sick are they?" Luke asked, concerned.

"No worse than anyone else who's had this flu. I

have them sucking on ice chips now. They were very calm about the whole thing."

"Well, I appreciate your being so responsible," Luke said, handing her some money.

"Hey, I don't charge this much."

"Sounds like you've earned every penny tonight. Let's go."

He walked a chattering Debbie home, then sprinted back to the house. Courtney was just coming down the stairs as he walked in the front door.

"Well?" he said.

"Debbie was right. She had everything under control. She changed their beds and pajamas, gave them ice chips to suck on. Jessica is asleep already, and Kevin won't be long."

"Lord, imagine being sick when your mother isn't home. That has to be scary as hell."

Courtney laughed. "They tossed their cookies quite nicely without me. Kevin was more interested in telling me about his new score on the computer game."

"Dammit, Courtney, this isn't funny. Do you realize Debbie had no way of reaching us?"

"Yes, that's my fault. I certainly won't let that happen again."

"While we were . . ." He began to pace the floor. "Those poor little kids were sick as dogs. That is so rotten."

"Excuse me," Courtney said, "but are we doing role reversal here? I'm the mother who went off and left her children for the evening. Why are you having a case of the guilts? I'm not."

"You're not?" he asked, stopping to look at her. "Why not? Your children threw up and you weren't even home."

"For heaven's sake, Luke," she said, planting her hands on her hips, "they've got the flu, not the bubonic plague. They're not even running fevers. They redistributed their junk food, that's all. I'll keep them quiet tomorrow, and that should be that."

"Parents should wear beepers, like doctors. They should pass a law saying all parents must wear beepers."

"Waterproof beepers. Just in case one decides to take a dip in a hot tub."

"Shh," Luke said, looking at the ceiling. "Don't say *hot tub* too loud. Kevin might hear you. We don't want to mess up his psyche. Kids understand a lot more than we realize."

"Thank you, Dr. Hamilton," she said dryly. "I can't believe this."

"And I can't believe how casually you're behaving about all this. How would you like to be two years old and only have a baby-sitter to throw up on? You should have been here, Courtney."

"Well, it's a little tough being in two places at once," she said, poking him in the chest with her finger. "I don't recall hearing any complaints from you earlier as to where I was."

"Don't get nasty," he said, narrowing his eyes.

"Then don't you dare tell me how to be a mother. I've been doing this for six years without your help, and I'll do it for many more without you. You've got a lot of nerve, do you know that?"

"Dammit, I care about those kids."

"And you're saying I don't because I took a few hours off to be a woman? Lord, you're infuriating. You don't have any concept of what it's like to be a mother. Or a father, for that matter. Don't pass judgment on me. Don't ever do that, Luke. Until you've walked in my shoes, don't tell me how to wear them."

"Look, I—"

"Go home," she said, wrapping her arms around herself. "I'm tired and I'd like to go to bed. Thank you for . . . everything."

"Ah, Courtney." He pulled her into his embrace. "I'm sorry. I was so off base it's a sin. I know you're a wonderful mother. I overreacted to Jessica and Kevin's being sick without you here. I'm really sorry. Hey." He tilted her chin up with one finger. "Forgive me?"

"Oh, Luke," she said, sighing. "Our worlds are just so different, so—"

"No, no," he interrupted. "No heavy talk tonight. We made beautiful love and beautiful memories. Let's savor them. I'm going to leave now, so you can get some sleep. I'd feel a helluva lot better if you said you'd forgiven me for barking at you, but I won't push my luck. Ahh, is that a smile I see creeping in around the edges?"

"No," she said, bursting into laughter. "You are such a con artist. You could talk yourself out of any kind of trouble."

"Charisma, darlin'," he said, lowering his head toward hers. "I took a course in charisma."

As Luke's mouth took possession of hers, Courtney gave up the battle and slid her arms around his waist. Their tongues met, and her knees began to tremble.

Suddenly an ear-splitting shriek reverberated through the air, and Courtney clutched Luke's shirt in fright as his head snapped up.

"Hooray!" Kevin yelled.

Courtney spun around, her eyes wide, heart racing. Her son was standing halfway down the stairs, whooping with joy.

"You did it, Mom! You kissed Luke, and Luke kissed you, just like I asked you to."

"Kevin, honey," she said, raising a hand, "listen to me. This doesn't mean—"

"Neato! Neato! Neato! Luke is going to be my dad. Me and Jessica are going to have the most neato dad in the whole wide world!"

Eight

Courtney had the irrational throught that if she closed her eyes, then opened them again, Kevin would have disappeared. It didn't work. Momentarily lacking the courage even to glance in Luke's direction, she walked to the bottom of the stairs.

"Kevin," she said firmly, "this is not the time to talk about this. I want you to go back to bed."

"But I—"

"Kevin, march."

" 'Kay," he said. And march he did, each thudding step punctuated with a decisive "Neato!"

Courtney turned slowly to face Luke. He had a rather pleasant, nondescript expression on his face, and his arms were crossed loosely over his chest.

"Kids are characters, aren't they?" she said with a weak smile. "Funny as a crutch."

"It would seem we have a problem."

"We?"

"I'm the neato dad, remember? Why don't I put on a pot of coffee and we'll discuss it?"

"Oh, that's not necessary," she said, waving her hand breezily. "By tomorrow Kevin will have forgotten all about this."

"Do you honestly believe that?"

"No," she said, sighing. "I don't."

"I'll make the coffee. Why don't you change into jeans or whatever is comfortable? It's not that late, Courtney."

"Yes, all right."

"Hey, don't look so down. You're not alone, you know. I'm right here with you."

But for how long? she wondered.

As Luke made the coffee, he felt like humming. Hell, he felt like singing from the rooftops. Kevin, his buddy Kevin, was in his corner. The most neato dad in the whole wide world? Holy smoke! This was unreal, fantastic.

But how to handle this? Luke pondered. It had to be done with finesse and tact. When a guy was handed an extra ace, he'd be a fool to waste it.

He poured coffee into mugs, then sat down at the table just as Courtney entered the kitchen. She had changed into jeans and a faded sweatshirt. Luke decided she was absolutely beautiful.

"Kevin go back to bed?" he asked as she sat down opposite him.

"Yes."

"I've heard him talk before about wanting to have a father. Would I be safe in saying he's chosen me for the job?"

"Yes," she said, frowning. "This is my fault. I should have talked to him before, but I was being selfish."

"What do you mean?"

"I was afraid he'd get his hopes up if I went out with you, but I wanted to go, so . . . Kevin really thinks that if people kiss each other they've made a commitment for life. In his mind, all it would take for you to become his father would be for us to share a kiss. Oh, dear, what a mess. I have a headache."

"That's understandable. You have a lot on your mind. Why don't you take some aspirin?"

"No, my stomach isn't that steady at the moment. I don't think it would appreciate having aspirin plopped in there. Oh, Luke, my heart aches for Kevin. He's old enough to have vague memories of Joe, of what it was like to have two parents. He wants a father so desperately, and I didn't have the courage to tell him it just isn't going to happen."

"Why isn't it?" Luke asked quietly.

"Well, you heard him. He's zeroed in on you."

"And, of course, you've canceled the husband hunt, deciding you don't need some yo-yo and his dirty socks."

"Something like that," she said, staring into her mug.

"Don't you think perhaps you should reconsider? Courtney, can you look me in the eye and say that you're comfortable having an affair?"

"We're not discussing that right now," she said, still staring into her mug. "Kevin is the subject."

"It's all tied in together," Luke said, catching one of her hands in his. "I know you, Courtney. You want to do what's best for those kids. In this instance, I believe that their needs match yours. They should have a father, and you should have a husband."

"Nice speech," she said, pulling her hand free, "but you keep forgetting that my son has made his choice as to who gets the dubious honor of assuming the father role around here."

"So he has. Can't picture Kevin settling for Leonard. After all, I'm neato. I must say, Kevin has excellent taste."

"Cute. I can do without your overinflated ego at the moment. Well, all I can do is sit Kevin down and explain the facts to him."

"Which are?"

"Are you purposely being dense? That child witnessed a kiss, which he interpreted to be second only to a wedding ceremony. I should have made it clear to him the night he begged me to kiss you, but he was so upset and . . . Well, the damage is done. He'll get over it in time. It's just that he lost one father and now . . . Oh, why, why, did I do this to him?"

"Take it easy, okay? You're being so damn hard on yourself. Courtney, there's something I think you should know." Okay, Hamilton, he thought, go for it. The rest of his life hinged on what he was about to say. He was going to ask the only woman he had ever loved to marry him. If he blew this, he'd shoot himself. "Courtney, I—"

"Excuse me," she said, slowly pushing herself out of her chair.

"Where in the hell are you going? This is important."

"I do believe I'm going to toss my cookies," she said, and ran out of the kitchen.

"I love you," Luke said dryly to the empty room. "Will you marry me? You will? Great. First rate. Oh, Lord." He jumped to his feet. "Courtney's sick."

He strode upstairs and knocked several times on her bathroom door.

"Courtney?"

"Oh-h-h, go away."

"No."

"I have the right to die in peace. Go away."

"Die? Don't you dare die," he said, flinging open the door.

Courtney was on the floor, her forehead resting on drawn-up knees. Luke hunkered down in front of her.

"You guys sure share around here," he said gently. "The flu bug snuck up on you, I guess. Do you think you've finished tossing your cookies?"

She nodded, but didn't move.

He stood up, scooped her into his arms, and carried her from the bathroom.

"What are you doing?" she said. "Oh-h-h, don't jiggle me. Every bone in my body aches."

"You belong in bed, and I'm taking you there."

"You can't do that. Put me down, dammit."

"Quit swearing. There are impressionable children in the house."

"But it's all right for you to carry me off to my bed?"

"Said impressionable children are asleep." He laid her down on her bed.

"Oh-h-h, my stomach, my head, my body."

"That about covers the inventory. Nightie. Oh, yeah, you kept it behind the bathroom door. Take your clothes off."

"I certainly will not."

"You will or I will," he said, shrugging. He retrieved her nightie from the bathroom. "Well?"

"Leave the room."

"Cripes, Courtney, I've seen—"

"Hush your mouth, and leave the room."

"Women are nuts," he said, stalking to the door. "You have five minutes."

Courtney glared at Luke's broad back, then slid cautiously off the bed, clutching her stomach. She shed her clothes, donned the nightie, then crawled between the cool sheets with a weary sigh.

What an incredible night, she thought, closing her eyes. So much had happened since she'd left the house with Luke. But she just couldn't sort it all through now. In the morning she'd tackle the problems facing her.

Her eyes popped open when she felt the mattress shift. Luke was sitting on the edge of the bed, looking anxiously at her.

"Think you can sleep?" he asked.

"No doubt about it. I'm exhausted."

"Can I get you anything? Water? Aspirin?"

"No, thank you."

"You're sure pale, Courtney."

"I feel pale," she said, closing her eyes again. "I'll be fine in the morning. Just need some sleep."

"Okay," he said, then leaned over and kissed her on the forehead.

"Be sure and lock the front door on your . . ." She yawned. ". . . way out."

"Got it. Good night, Courtney."

" 'Night," she said, then rolled onto her side, her back to him.

Luke turned off the light and stood up, shoving his hands into his back pockets. His eyes adjusted to the darkness, and he stared down at Courtney. She sighed and curled her hand next to her cheek. He smiled.

She looked like a little girl, he thought. But Courtney Marshall was definitely a woman, his woman. She was his love, his life, his future wife. She was the mother of two children he yearned to raise as his own, and the mother of the babies they would create together. She was Courtney.

"What tangled webs we weave," he said quietly. Everything was going to work out fine, he told himself. It just had to. Without Courtney he'd be so damn lonely. And he was really, really tired of being lonely.

He tucked the blankets around her shoulders, trailed his thumb lightly across her cheek, and left the room. He checked on both Jessica and Kevin, then opened a door in the hall that he hoped was to a linen closet. He found a blanket and a pillow, and headed back downstairs with them under his arm. After locking up the house, he turned off the lights, tugged off his shoes, and stretched out on the sofa.

There was no way he was going home, he'd decided. His family was ill and they needed him. His family? Damn right. That was exactly what they were. Now if he could convince Courtney of that, he'd be in good shape.

"I can't lose her," he said into the darkness. "I love them all. I need them all."

He rubbed his hand over his face, then sighed deeply and forced himself to relax. A few minutes later he drifted off to sleep.

Courtney stirred, realized her head ached, and foggily decided not to wake up after all.

"Mom?" came a loud whisper.

"Hmm?" she said, not opening her eyes.

"I'm supposed to see if you're awake, 'cause Luke's gonna bring you tea, and junk, if you are."

"That's nice," she murmured dreamily. "What?" she said an instant later, sitting bolt upright in bed and staring at Kevin. "Luke is what? Oh, my head."

"Gonna fix you breakfast."

She glanced at the clock. "It's nine o'clock? Nine? Where's Jessica?"

"In the kitchen with Luke. He got her dressed, and stuff. We had toast and scrambled eggs. Me and Jessica aren't sick any more."

"What time did Luke come over? Did you let him in?"

"Nope, he was sleeping on the sofa when I waked up."

"He was what? He spent the night here? Oh, good Lord."

"Neato, huh? Just like a real dad. I'm so glad Luke's gonna be my dad. I gotta go tell him you waked up."

"Kevin, wait," Courtney said, but Kevin had already dashed from the room. "Oh-h-h," she moaned, sinking back against the pillow. "Is Luke out of his mind? How could he do this to me? Now Kevin . . . Oh, I'm going to strangle that man."

Muttering under her breath, she shuffled into the bathroom, washed her face, brushed her teeth, and decided she felt as though she'd run five miles. She glanced in the mirror, rolled her eyes in disgust at her pale reflection, then crawled back into bed.

A minute later Luke entered the room carrying a tray. " 'Morning. Tea, toast, sliced peaches. Prop yourself up against the pillow."

"No."

"Courtney, this isn't up for a vote. Do it."

She shot him a stormy glare, but did as she was instructed. He placed the tray across her thighs, then grasped her wrist between his fingers and thumb as he looked at his watch.

"What are you doing?" she asked.

"Taking your pulse."

"Why?"

He shrugged. "I don't know. In the movies they always take the patient's pulse."

"Oh, for Pete's sake," she said, wiggling her arm free.

"Eat," he said, pointing to the tray. He sprawled into a chair and casually crossed one ankle over his knee. "I'll watch you. Oh, I borrowed your razor. Eat."

"No. Luke, why did you spend the night here? Don't you realize you've only made things worse as far as Kevin is concerned?"

"That was a risk I had to run. I couldn't leave, knowing you were sick."

"You couldn't?"

"Of course not."

"Of course not?"

"Do you have any close relatives who are parrots? Eat."

"It's a very nice breakfast," she said. "Thank you."

"All part of the service."

"Service?"

"Would you stop that? Eat something."

She took a sip of tea, then nibbled on a piece of toast.

"By the way," Luke said, "your mother called."

She nearly choked. "From Florida?"

"You have more than one mother?"

"No. You answered the phone? What did you tell her?"

"I said you were still in bed and could I take a message."

"You didn't," she said, shaking her head. "Tell me you didn't say that."

"It's not nice to lie to mothers. I felt honor bound to tell the truth. She, of course, was a tad curious as to who I was."

"This ought to be good," Courtney said. "Who are you? Or who were you when you told her who you were, or . . . I'm confusing myself."

"All I said was that you had the flu and I was helping out."

"Thank goodness for that much," she said, and took another bite of toast.

"Of course Kevin blew that story when he got on and told her I was going to be his neato dad."

"Aagh!" Courtney shrieked. "How could you have allowed him to do that?"

"How in the hell did I know what he was going to say? The kid wanted to talk to his grandmother, so I let him. Jessica had her turn too. She said 'Lu' six times. Your mom sounds like a nice lady. Gentleman that I am, I got back on the line and told her that there was a very reasonable explanation for all of this, and—"

"And?"

"—and as soon as we figured out what it was, you'd call her back and explain."

"Oh-h-h," Courtney moaned.

"She fell apart. Your mom came unglued, she was laughing so hard. She said something about its being long overdue, then had to hang up because she got the hiccups from laughing. Nifty person, your mom. I like her."

"I'm having a relapse," Courtney said, covering her eyes with her hand.

"No kidding?" Luke said, leaning forward. "There are two aspirin on your tray there. You'd better take them."

"Yes." She gulped them down with the tea. "I'll get up and— "

"No way. You aren't moving. I have everything under control."

"But we have to talk about Kevin, about—"

"Later." He lifted the tray off her legs. "You sleep some more."

"Luke," Kevin said, running into the room, "I was trying to pour Jessica some orange juice, but I dropped the jug. There's orange juice on the floor and the cupboards, oh, and all over Jessica."

"Oh, dear," Courtney said, tossing back the blankets.

"Halt," Luke said, raising his hand. "Get back in there. I'll handle this."

"A toddler and a kitchen that has been redecorated with orange juice?"

"What do you think I am? Stupid? I do know how to scrub, Courtney. Come on, Kevin, show me where the mop is. I'm being insulted in this room. Hey, we'd better grab some clean clothes for Jessica while we're up here, sport."

" 'Kay."

Courtney smiled and shook her head, then sank back against the pillow. Oh, how she loved Luke Hamilton, she mused. He was being so wonderful. It had been a long time since she'd been pampered and cared for. He was acting like a husband and father, with no questions asked.

But, she had to admit, the situation was unique, because she had the flu. As soon as she was better, she was sure Luke would fall over his feet getting back to the peace and quiet of his plush home. But for now it was heavenly having Luke here, being her partner, helping her through a crisis. Talking to her mother.

Courtney frowned. Oh, yes, she could well imagine her mother thoroughly enjoying the juicy scene she'd inadvertently stumbled into with her call. She'd immediately share the news with Courtney's father that there was, at last, a man once again in their daughter's life. Darn, more people to be disappointed when Luke disappeared into thin air.

And he had to go, Courtney decided. She would not be allowed any more stolen hours with Luke Hamilton because of Kevin. She would have to tell her son that Luke was not going to be his dad. Then Luke had to get out of their lives so that Kevin's wounds could heal. She'd nap now and talk to Luke later. Say good-bye to Luke. Forever.

With a wobbly sigh Courtney rolled onto her stomach and closed her eyes, ignoring the tears that slid down her cheeks.

Over two hours later Luke sat down at the kitchen table, a mug of coffee in his hand and a frown on his face.

The mothers of America, he decided, deserved the Congressional Medal of Honor for Valor, Bravery, and Endurance, and a hunk of money for hazardous-duty pay. Statues should be erected in their honor in every city park across the country. The president should invite them all to the White House for dinner. And orange juice should be banned, wiped off the face of the earth.

He had walked in Courtney's shoes, and he was in awe. Exhausted and in awe.

Well, he thought, one thing was for sure. When he and Courtney were married he was going to hire a woman to help her. He had a housekeeper who came in twice a week, and she might be convinced to take on the extra work if he paid her more. Maybe he'd ask her to come in every day. Yes, good idea, he decided. He had a slew of modern appliances in his kitchen. Kevin would love the crushed ice zooming from the refrigerator door. He'd put a latch high on the outside of his and Courtney's bedroom door so there'd be no chance of Jessica or Kevin's falling into the hot tub. His and Courtney's bedroom, he repeated silently. Their private place, for just the two of them, man and woman, husband and wife. They'd make love there, exquisite love, at night, at dawn, whenever they could sneak away. And they'd talk and share. They'd laugh, make plans for the future, create lists of names for their babies yet to come. And they'd never be lonely.

It was going to be so good, all of it. He wanted that life with Courtney. He wanted it so damn bad, it caused a cold ache in his gut even to consider it might not come to be. He had to talk to her. Now.

"Luke," Kevin said, running into the kitchen, "can we have lunch? I sure am hungry."

"Lunch?" He looked at Kevin rather blankly. "Already? Yeah, I guess it's about that time. Okay, get Jessica, and you guys wash your hands. I'll see what I can put together."

" 'Kay."

Lunch was a haphazardly accomplished feat, and an hour later the kitchen was once again in order, Kevin was engrossed in a computer game, and Jessica was in her crib for a nap. Luke met Courtney as she came out of her bedroom.

"You're dressed," he said, his gaze sweeping over her jeans and yellow knit top. "Why are you out of bed?"

"Because I feel fine," she said, smiling at him. "Good as new. I slept the morning away, and I'm fit as a fiddle. Hungry, too. Thank you so much, Luke. Oh, that's not even close to adequate."

"True," he said, drawing her into his arms. "I deserve a kiss for my war efforts against the orange-juice enemy."

"Who won?"

"I did, of course. But you see an older and wiser man before you, Ms. Marshall. My respect and admiration for the mothers of this world has increased tenfold."

"How nice," she said, laughing.

"I mean it, Courtney. Those shoes of yours are gigantic. I'm not sure there's a man who can fill them steadily. Yes, this weary soldier needs a kiss to rejuvenate his battered body and mind. I cannot believe how many questions Kevin can ask in the span of one hour. And Jessica, bless her heart, seems to need to drag out all of her toys before she can decide which to play with. And—"

"Oh, you poor dear," Courtney said, placing her hand on his face. "I'll kiss you and make it better."

"Now you're talking. I need some mouth-to-mouth resuscitation."

The kiss was sweet and sensuous, but to Courtney, much too short.

"We need to talk," Luke said when he lifted his head.

No! Courtney thought frantically. Not now. Not

yet. Later. To talk was to face the hopelessness of their relationship and the danger to Kevin's and perhaps even Jessica's mental well-being. To talk was to end it all and say good-bye. No, she didn't want to talk, she wanted to make love with Luke. She wanted to feel, not think, to soar beyond the here and now and not face reality.

"Yes," she said quietly, "we have to talk."

"Let's get some food in you. No one can carry on a heavy discussion on an empty stomach."

She managed to produce a weak smile, and they went down the stars. She greeted Kevin, then told Luke she was officially back on duty and would make her own lunch. She heated soup on the lowest temperature on the stove, postponing for as long as possible the moment when she would sit across the table from Luke for the last time.

"Did you eat?" she asked, finally sitting down with her soup.

"Yep."

"The kitchen looks great. No one would ever know it had an orange-juice bath."

"Spit-shined. Shovel in that soup while it's hot. Did you call your mother back."

"No, not yet."

"Good. We need to talk first."

Courtney nodded, unable to speak past the lump in her throat as she stared into the bowl of steaming soup.

"Courtney," Luke started, then drew a deep steadying breath. "I'm very honored that Kevin thinks I'd made a neato dad. Jessica seems to like me too."

"Yes. Yes, she does," Courtney said, still not looking at him.

"'You once told me that you'd have to love a man

to make love with him. Of course, that was during the husband-hunt phase. You and I made love when we were supposedly engaged in an affair."

"Supposedly?" she said, looking up at him quickly.

"Okay, having, starting, our affair. Thing is, I really need to know if you changed your mind about having to be in love to make love when you canceled the husband hunt."

"What difference does it make?"

"A helluva lot of difference," he said, smacking the table. Courtney's soup sloshed over the edge of her bowl. "Sorry. Look, let me start over. The fact that Kevin and Jessica like me is very important, and eliminates one entire area of potential problems. You've had them longer than you've had me, so it's understandable that they have rank. But I'm neato, so that only leaves finding out where *you're* coming from."

"No, it leaves trying to figure out what you're saying. You're not making any sense, Luke."

"I'm not?"

"No."

"Damn," he said, running his hand through his hair.

"Luke, I can't ignore what Kevin believes to be true about us. It would be very cruel to allow him to think you're going to be his father."

"But I am!"

She blinked once, slowly. "I beg your pardon?" she said.

"That's what I've been trying to get out of my fumble mouth, don't you see? I *am* going to be Kevin and Jessica's father, the neato dad. Courtney, I love you. I love you, and I want to marry you, have you marry me, have us get married. I love you, and Kevin and Jessica, I swear I do."

"What?" she whispered. "'You what?"

"I love you," he said, taking her hands in his. "But here's the biggy. Do *you* love *me?* Oh, please, Courtney, tell me you love me. Tell me you'll marry me. Please? I'll sign a document in blood stating I'll never leave my dirty socks on the floor. Please?"

Courtney didn't know how she got onto Luke's lap. She had no idea if she'd gone over, under, or around the table, but she was suddenly there, flinging her arms around his neck as tears spilled onto her cheeks.

"Oh, Luke, I love you so much," she said, her voice trembling. "I never dreamed that you . . . I knew you cared for me, and I was hoping, praying, that you'd . . . But I ran out of time, because Kevin saw us kissing and . . . Yes, I love you. Yes, I'll marry you. You'll be the most neato husband and father in the whole wide world."

"Courtney," he said with a groan, then cupped her head in his hands and brought her mouth to his.

The kiss was urgent, frenzied. They drank deeply of each other. Luke dropped his hands to Courtney's back to press her close to him, crushing her breasts against his chest. She leaned further into him, savoring his heat, his strength, the evidence of his arousal. Desire swirled within her. She needed to touch and be touched. She ached to be consumed by all that was Luke.

"Courtney," he said, his voice gritty, "our son— Lord, I love the way that sounds—our son is liable to come charging in here any minute. Kissing is one thing, but this is a bit much."

"Yes, of course," she said, her own voice shaky. "Oh, Luke, I'm so happy."

"Lady, the word *happy* just doesn't cut it for the way I'm feeling. I love you. I love you, Courtney, and if even one day in our lives goes by and I forget to tell you, pop me in the chops."

"Okay," she said, laughing.

"Now, get back over there and eat your soup before we get in real trouble here."

"Yes, sir," she said, sliding off his lap.

"I like your attitude."

She sent him a mock glare as she sat down and picked up her spoon.

"Courtney, would you be willing to have a baby, my baby? I mean, our baby?"

"Yes," she said, smiling warmly.

"Two?"

"Well . . ."

"Three?"

"Don't push your luck, Hamilton."

"Oh. Well, we'll have them one at a time, and see how it goes. We should get the show on the road, though, so they'll grow up together. Right? I'm telling you, I've got so many great plans for us."

"Oh?" she said.

"We'll get married as soon as possible, then move the crew to my place. I know it's a big house, but you won't have to mess with it. I'll hire a housekeeper to take care of everything. In fact, it wouldn't hurt to get you help with the cooking."

"But—"

"I already have a gardener, so don't even give a thought to having to tend to those lawns and flowers. Oh, and your days of typing until midnight are over. You won't have to do that any more. You'll need to notify your clients that you're no longer in business. Then—"

"Luke, wait a minute," she said, raising her hand. "On the surface this sounds marvelous, and I certainly appreciate everything you're suggesting. But you haven't left me anything to do."

"You'll be a wife and mother."

"Yes, but—"

"It's going to be great, you'll see. Let's tell Kevin now, all right? Then we've got to call your folks, Anne and Larry . . . Hell, the world! I'll go get Kevin, okay?"

"Yes, fine," she said absently, but he had already left the kitchen. What was wrong with her? she wondered. Her dream had come true. Luke loved her, wanted to marry her and be a father to her children. Yet she had a strange feeling of apprehension. Luke wanted to give her so much. No, *too* much. That was what was wrong—the image in her mind of herself sitting in that enormous house with nothing to do. Well, no problem. She'd simply explain to him that as the wife, the mother, the homemaker, *she* tended to her own chores. Okay. Everything was perfect, absolutely wonderful. "Neato," she said with a smile.

Nine

The wedding was to take place one month from the Saturday that Luke had proposed to Courtney in her kitchen.

Everyone they had called that day had been ecstatic over the news. Kevin had shouted his approval in fifteen nonstop "neatos," and Jessica had clapped her hands, although Courtney was sure the toddler had no idea what was going on.

Courtney would have preferred a simple ceremony in a judge's chambers, but she agreed to the much larger affair that Luke wanted, since he had never been married before. A printer friend of Luke's promised to rush the invitations, and Courtney made a list of friends she wanted to invite. She asked Luke for his list so that she could get the invitations addressed and in the mail as quickly as possible.

"Marsha is going to do that," he said. "Oh, and the reception arrangements are all set. Marsha was recently married, you know. She's a pro at this. You don't have to think about a thing."

"Oh," Courtney said.

She gave two weeks' notice to the companies she did typing for, and the secretaries moaned at the news that they were losing such efficient help. The final typing assignments from each were twice the normal size, and Courtney began staying up well past midnight to work.

"You should have just quit cold," Luke told her. "I don't like your working this hard. You notice that L and L didn't ask for one last shot."

"I wanted to do this right," Courtney said. "I've established a good reputation, and I can't just disappear into thin air. It won't hurt me to push for a while."

"Well, I'll be glad when that computer is used for nothing more than the kids' games," he said.

"Oh," she said again.

They agreed that Courtney's house should be put up for sale, and the money from the sale would be placed in accounts to be used when Jessica and Kevin went to college. One morning Courtney woke to the sound of men's voices, and discovered a crew was painting the outside of the house. She immediately called Luke.

"Yeah, I know," he said. "I'm sprucing up the place a bit before we put it on the market."

"You could have told me."

"You have enough to do without worrying about peeling paint. I'll handle all of the details about the house. Don't even think about it."

"Oh."

Three days after that, Courtney's mother called.

"I'll make it quick, dear," she said. "Your father

and I have decided we'd like to take the children to Disneyland while you're away. We wanted your permission so we could make the hotel reservations."

"Away?" Courtney said. "Away where?"

"Oh, no, have I spilled the beans? I assumed you and Luke had discussed your honeymoon trip to Hawaii. Now I've done it. Can you still act surprised when he tells you? Oh, and may we take Jessica and Kevin to Disneyland?"

"Yes. Yes, of course," Courtney said absently. "That's very generous of you."

"We'll have such fun. Well, see you soon, dear. Oh, Courtney, I'm just so happy for you and Luke and the children. I've always hated the thought of your being alone. You need a husband."

"Oh. Well, I—"

"We're counting the days until the wedding. 'Bye for now."

"Yes. Good-bye," Courtney said. She immediately called Luke. "Hawaii?" she said, after Marsha connected her with him.

"Damn, who squealed?"

"My mother assumed I knew. They want to take the kids to Disneyland while we're away?"

"Hey, that's great. They'll love Disneyland."

"Luke, when did you plan to tell me we were going to Hawaii?" Courtney asked, squeezing the bridge of her nose.

"When we got on the plane. It was supposed to be a surprise."

"Oh, it would have been a surprise, all right," she said dryly. "I wouldn't have had any luggage."

"I know. I planned to buy you all new things once we got there. I'm still going to do it that way."

"Don't be silly. I have perfectly fine clothes."

"Hey, I want to do this for you. After the wedding reception, we'll just walk out the door. You won't have to think about packing or anything. I've got to go now, Courtney. I'm due in a meeting. I love you."

"I love you too," she said softly, but she knew she was frowning.

Luke began to put in long hours at L and L to complete a bid on a large contract, so that he wouldn't leave Larry in a bind. Courtney finished the last of the typing assignments, then began the tedious chore of sorting through years' of accumulated possessions. Her conversations with Luke became hurried exchanges on the telephone. The painting of the house was finished, and a realtor placed a "For Sale" sign on the front lawn.

Anne and Larry had insisted on taking Courtney and Luke out for a celebration dinner at one of the finest restaurants in Carmel. Courtney immediately liked Luke's sister and brother-in-law, and felt welcomed into the family.

"Mom and Dad are cutting their trip short to the Virgin Islands to be here for the wedding," Luke said.

"That's good," Anne said. "You're going to have to be firm with our parents, Courtney, or they'll spoil Jessica and Kevin rotten."

"I'll speak to them," Luke said before Courtney could reply. "Courtney doesn't need to be worrying about her in-laws. You're rather quiet, Courtney. Do you feel all right?"

"Yes, I'm fine. I'm tired, that's all. There's so much sorting and packing to do."

The next day, Saturday, three teenagers showed up at Courtney's. They were the children of friends of Luke's, and Luke had hired them to help her sort and pack. Courtney rolled her eyes and waved the youths into the house.

As the days passed, Courtney grew increasingly edgy and tense. Her once-orderly home was strewn with boxes, which had to be taped shut to keep Jessica from emptying them. The majority of her furniture had been purchased by a young married couple, leaving little to sit on. They moved the computer to Kevin's new room at Luke's, only to have Kevin complain that he was bored without it and ask why they couldn't go live at Luke's right now.

Feeling like a total idiot, Courtney had to telephone Marsha to ask what shade the flowers on the altar were going to be, so that she could purchase her dress. She didn't want to clash horribly with the color scheme.

"Oh, didn't Luke tell you?" Marsha said. "It's all done in dusty rose and pink. I've ordered your bouquet and corsages for the mothers. Would you like a piece of ribbon so you can match your and Jessica's dresses?"

"Fine," Courtney said wearily.

The ribbon sample was delivered by messenger. Courtney gritted her teeth and went shopping for the dresses.

On one of the few nights that Courtney and Luke were able to schedule a few hours for themselves, Courtney fell asleep on his bed after dinner while he was showering. Luke sat on the edge of the bed with a towel wrapped around his waist and kissed her awake.

"What?" Courtney said foggily. "Oh, goodness, I'm sorry. I must have dozed off."

"I'm worried about you," Luke said. "You look so tired. You're trying to do too much, Courtney."

"Luke, I'm not doing anything! Everything is being taken care of by you or people you've hired."

"Then why are you so beat? Do you think you should see a doctor?"

"No, I'm not sick. It's just . . . I don't know. Everything seems so out of control. It's hard to explain. I feel as though I'm on the outside looking in and . . . Oh, darn, I'm going to cry."

"Hey, easy," he said, stretching out next to her. "You've got the prewedding jitters. This is Thursday, my love. By this time Saturday you'll be Mrs. Luke Hamilton, and we'll be winging our way to Hawaii. Sound good?"

"Yes," she said, and sniffled. "Luke, make love with me, please? I just want to think about you, me, us right now."

"Oh, lady, it will be my pleasure. This is your night, Courtney. I want to do this for you, give to you. Give and give."

But it was Courtney who took charge.

In a bold move that surprised herself as well as Luke, she slid off the bed and slowly removed her clothes. Each garment was drawn seductively from her body as Luke's eyes became smoky with desire. His sharp intake of breath as she slid her bikini panties down her slender legs told of his rising passion.

He lunged to his feet, only to have Courtney step back out of his reach. His hands curled into tight fists as she moved closer, then pulled his towel free and dropped it onto the floor. The slow, sensual look she slid over his entire body caused his manhood to stir with hunger for her. Then, with fluttering kisses, flickering tongue, nibbling teeth, caressing hands, she explored every inch of him.

"Courtney . . ." Luke groaned, trying to control his trembling.

"Don't you like this, Luke?" she murmured.

"Yes. It's fantastic. You're fantastic. I can't take . . . much more, though, Courtney. I . . . oh, Courtney, stop. I want to do this for you too."

"No, not tonight. *I'm* making love to you. *I'm* having a say. I'm important." Tears spilled onto her cheeks. "I'm capable of pleasing you. I'm a woman, your woman, and I'm showing you just how much of a woman I am."

Through the hazy, passion-laden fog that enveloped Luke he realized something was wrong. Courtney was crying, and there was a frantic edge to her voice. He tried to think of what he should say to find out what was wrong, but only a groan erupted from his lips as she continued to work her magic.

They tumbled onto the bed, but Courtney still reigned supreme. She straddled Luke's body and settled over his surging manhood, bringing a moan of pleasure rumbling up from his chest. He gripped her tiny waist in his large hands and they began to move with a thundering cadence, a tempo that increased to a pounding rhythm. Courtney threw her head back as the pinnacle was reached, and then Luke arched his body to drive deep into her and complete his climb.

She collapsed against him, spent, gasping for breath. He held her tightly to him, their bodies moist from exertion, hearts beating wildly. Courtney slowly lifted her lashes, then started to move off Luke.

"Don't go," he protested, his voice raspy.

"I'll smash you."

"No, I don't think so, featherweight," he said, smiling.

"Okay," she said with a contented sigh. "I'll stay right here. You're really quite comfortable to rest on, considering you're so muscle-bound."

"Oh, thanks."

"That was a compliment."

"I'll take your word for it. Courtney? Is something wrong? Besides prewedding jitters?"

"No. I'll be fine after we get settled in here, Luke, you'll see. Everything has been hectic. But it's almost over, and we'll soon be on the beach in Hawaii. Heavenly. I love you so much, Luke."

"And I love you, Courtney mine. Lord, how I love you."

They lay in silence, each lost in his own thoughts. Then Luke glanced at the clock. His dejected sigh and well-chosen expletive told her it was time to go home.

"At least we're in the countdown," he said as he reached for his clothes. "It's measured off in hours now. This has been a helluva long month."

"Yes, it certainly has," she said, sliding off the bed. "I wouldn't want to go through it again, that's for sure."

"Well, all the hassle will be well worth it. We'll be married, have our honeymoon, then start living a normal life together. This house will be a home because of you, our love, Jessica, and Kevin."

"Speaking of those kids," she said, "I cringe at the thought of their clambering all over your expensive furniture. They're not naughty, but they're definitely busy."

"Hey," he said, pulling her into his arms, "those are *our* kids climbing on *our* furniture. When they wear it out, get some more. You're the boss about that stuff."

Courtney smiled. Thank goodness, she thought. At least Luke had given up his harebrained plan to hire half the world to come in and help her run the home. He hadn't mentioned it since the day he proposed.

"What's that smile for?" he asked.

"Just counting the hours until I'm your wife."

He took her into his arms. "You are my life," he said, "my reason for being. Thank you, Courtney, for loving me, for trusting me with your love, for believing in me enough to allow me to be a father to your children."

"You're going to make me cry again."

"Brides sure cry a lot."

"Oh, yeah, Hamilton? Wait until I'm pregnant. I'm a weepy mess for nine months."

"I'm geared up," he said, smiling. "You checked with the doctor, right? You threw away your pills, right? We might be pregnant this very minute, right?"

"Right," she said, laughing.

"This house—no, this *home*—is going to ring with laughter and love."

"Yes. Yes, it will."

"And no one will ever be lonely," Luke said, lowering his lips to hers.

At four o'clock on Saturday afternoon, with over a hundred family members and friends as witnesses, Courtney and Luke exchanged vows and gold wedding bands and became husband and wife.

"You may kiss your wife," the minister said to Luke.

"I love you, Courtney," Luke said, and kissed her gently on the lips.

Tears filled her eyes. "And I love you, Luke."

They walked to the first pew, where Luke lifted Kevin into his arms and Courtney picked up Jessica. The four returned to the front of the church to stand facing the congregation, and the minister placed his hands on Courtney's and Luke's shoulders.

"Friends," he said, "may I present to you Mr. and Mrs. Lucas Hamilton and family. God bless them all."

Then, despite Courtney's many lectures on the subject, Kevin threw his arms around Luke's neck and cut loose with a jubilant "Neato!" that rang to the rafters of the old church. The outburst produced a round of applause and many tears from their friends and family.

The following hours were a blur to Courtney. The photographer Luke had hired gave orders like a drill sergeant for a seemingly endless number of pictures. Then Luke hustled her and the children into a limousine driven by Larry, and they were whisked away to a huge hotel where the reception was to be held. Courtney smiled and shook hands with so many people whom she didn't know, they simply became a sea of faces. She even had trouble remembering the names of the friends she'd invited and had known for years. The photographer continued to hover around, and was directing traffic while Courtney and Luke cut the many-tiered cake. They toasted each other with champagne once, then did it again when the man wanted a picture from another angle.

Luke's mother and father were warm and outgoing. They hugged Courtney and welcomed her into the family.

"Grandchildren," Mrs. Hamilton said with a wistful sigh. "I finally have grandchildren. I'm so eager to get to know Jessica and Kevin."

Courtney's mother joined them. "Would you like to see pictures of them when they were babies?" she asked. "I have a grandmother's brag book in my purse."

"Oh, I'd be delighted," Mrs. Hamilton said.

As the two sets of parents huddled together, Luke steered Courtney in the direction of the dance floor.

"Our kids are stealing the show," he said, chuckling.

"Your parents are marvelous."

"So are yours. And so are you."

The band began to play, and the crowd moved back to watch the bride and groom dance the first waltz.

"Some party, huh?" Luke said, as he led her with practiced ease.

"Yes. Yes, it is," she said, smiling slightly. "I feel as though I'm part of a Hollywood production, as if it's happening to someone else."

"It's all for real, my love. You are my wife. Oh, that sounds good. I really had my doubts for a while, there, that I'd be able to convince you to marry me. I'm going to spend the rest of my life making you happy, Courtney. Everything I have, everything I am, is yours."

Fresh tears spilled onto Courtney's cheeks, which brought a collective sigh of approval from the watching throng. Luke chuckled and pulled her closer. At last the song ended, and as the next one started, the floor became crowded with dancing couples.

For the next hour Courtney and Luke danced, mingled, and, of course, had their pictures taken. Suddenly Anne appeared at Luke's elbow.

"It's time," she said, tapping her watch.

"Great," Luke said. "Courtney, go with Anne for a minute, okay?"

"Why?"

"Trust me, new sister," Anne said, linking her arm through Courtney's.

In a beautifully decorated powder room, Anne drew a pale blue linen suit and a darker blue silk blouse from a garment bag. In a box were black leather pumps and a matching purse.

"Your traveling outfit," Anne said. "I hope you like it."

"Oh, Anne, it's beautiful," Courtney said, reverently taking the suit and blouse from Anne. "I've never had anything so elegant."

"I scoured the boutiques for it. Luke told me it had to be perfect."

"Anne, he's taking me off to Hawaii and I don't have one thing of my own with me. Not even my toothbrush."

"I know," Anne said, sighing. "I tried to talk him out of this ridiculous plan. I told him that a woman likes to have her own personal items, cosmetics, undies, things like that, with her. Stubborn Lucas insists on buying you all new things. Here, let me unzip your dress."

"I don't want to sound ungrateful, but . . . Oh, it's hard to explain. This past month has been a strain, I guess. Luke kept taking charge of things I would have preferred to handle myself, and—Darn it, I do sound ungrateful."

"No, Courtney, you don't. You sound like a capable, intelligent woman, who has been run over by a bulldozer in the form of Lucas Hamilton. Be patient with him, Courtney. He loves you so much, and he'd give you the moon and stars if he could. He'll get the hang of this husband number. If he doesn't, whop him up 'side the head."

The two women laughed, and Anne gave Courtney a quick hug. The suit fit perfectly, and Courtney blinked several times in amazement as she turned back and forth in front of the mirror.

"Good heavens, I'm gorgeous," she said, smiling brightly.

"Of course," Anne said. "You're a Hamilton. Now! Go give kisses to your kids, the moms and dads, then you and Luke scoot out of here. You've got a plane to catch. And Courtney?"

"Yes?"

"I'm so glad you love my brother. You and those precious children of yours are the best things that have ever happened to him. Be happy."

"Oh, I'm going to cry again."

Good-byes were said in a flurry of excitement. Then they dashed to Luke's sports car in a shower of rice.

"We did it," Courtney said, after waving to Jessica and Kevin out the window. "We escaped."

"Alone at last," Luke said, wiggling his eyebrows. "By the way, you look sensational, Mrs. Hamilton."

"Thank you, Mr. Hamilton. So do you."

"The next week is ours. It's going to be perfect, Courtney."

And it was.

It was everything and more than Courtney might have fantasized about in a whimsical, romantic moment. They made love at night and in the glow of dawn's light. They strolled along quiet beaches in the moonlight, ate wonderful, exotic food, and shopped until Courtney claimed her feet would never be the same. They toured the islands, attended a luau, swam and sunned. The magical days and nights passed all too quickly, and on Sunday afternoon they pulled into the driveway of their home.

Hours later they made love in what was now their bedroom. They'd heard a blow-by-blow description of Disneyland from Kevin, given up the battle and allowed Jessica to wear her Mickey Mouse ears to bed, and Luke had driven Courtney's parents to the airport.

"Good night, my wife," he said now, kissing her on the forehead. "Welcome home."

" 'Night," she said sleepily, snuggling closer to his warmth. "Welcome home to you too. I love . . . you . . ." Her voice trailed off.

Luke tightened his hold on her and listened to her quiet breathing. Then, with a contented sigh, he drifted off to sleep.

The next sound to penetrate Courtney's consciousness was Jessica's piercing scream. Courtney flung back the blankets, grabbed her new satin robe, and headed for the door. She absently realized that Luke had not been in bed and that the house was awash with sunlight. She ran down the hall to Jessica's room and nearly fell over Kevin, who was just inside the door.

"Don't touch my baby," Courtney said to the enormous woman standing by the crib. "Take anything else you want, but don't you dare lay a hand on my children."

The woman puffed herself up to an even greater size and glared at Courtney.

"Mrs. Hamilton," she said, her voice cool, "I highly resent the implication that I am a common thief."

Courtney rushed to the crib and snatched up a

whimpering Jessica, who was clutching her mouse ears in both hands.

"Then who are you?" Courtney asked "How did you get in here? What do you want?"

"I, madam, am Ethel Rosenbloom, your house-keeper."

"My who?"

"I previously worked two days a week for Mr. Hamilton, but he asked me over a month ago to start coming in every day beginning on this date. He was here when I arrived this morning, and informed me that I was to feed the children and allow you to sleep. But surely you were expecting me today."

"'No," Courtney said through clenched teeth, "I was not expecting you today, or any other day. I knew nothing of these arrangements."

"I see. Well, now you do know. I understand that Kevin will be returning to school next week, after spring break. I only agreed to watch one child during the day. Give me Jessica, and I'll prepare their breakfast."

"No! No! No!" Jessica shrieked, clinging to her mother as Ethel reached for her.

"Mrs. Rosenbloom—"

"Miss."

"Ethel. I'm afraid there's been a mistake. You see, I won't be needing a housekeeper, because I intend to take care of my family and this home myself."

"But Mr. Hamilton—"

"Mr. Hamilton," Courtney interrupted, "made a slight error. Now, if you'll come with me I'll give you a check to compensate for the inconvenience."

The check did wonders to smooth Ethel Rosenbloom's feathers, and Courtney closed the door behind her with a sigh of relief.

"That was a scary lady, Mom," Kevin said.

"Well, she's gone now," Courtney said. "Come on. I'll make breakfast."

Courtney frowned more than she smiled that day. She knew Luke would be unable to call her, since he and Larry were scheduled to be in a day-long meeting with several overseas pharmaceutical distributors.

How would Luke react when he found out she'd dismissed Ethel? she wondered. Well, she wasn't going to budge on this one. Luke had had his own way on every decision during the past month. But not this time, by golly. This was their home, and she was going to take care of it. And no woman, especially one who probably had been a discus thrower in her former life and who scared little kids half out of their minds, was coming within ten feet of their children.

The aroma of baking chicken greeted Luke when he entered the house shortly after five that evening.

"I'm home," he called. He was home, he repeated silently. It *was* a home.

Courtney smiled as she came out of the kitchen and saw Jessica and Kevin fling themselves at Luke. He lifted them one at a time above his head. Then they dashed off down the hall to watch "Mr. Rogers."

"My turn?" Courtney asked, walking toward him.

He pulled her into his arms. "I have more grown-up plans for you," he said, and took possession of her mouth in a long, searing kiss. "I missed you today," he said when he lifted his head. "Everything go okay?"

"Why don't you change out of that suit into something more comfortable; then we can talk. Dinner won't be ready for another half an hour."

"I shall return," he said. He kissed her quickly, then strode into the bedroom.

"He'd better not holler at me about Earthquake Ethel," Courtney said under her breath. "He'd just better not."

Luke returned dressed in jeans and a blue sweater, then asked Courtney if she'd like a drink before dinner.

"No, thank you," she said.

"I'll pass, too, I guess." He sat down on the sofa. "Come snuggle up here."

"Luke," she said, still standing several feet away from him, "I have to tell you something."

"Oh? Okay, what is it?"

"I fired Ethel Rosenbloom."

Luke came flying off the sofa so fast the Courtney jumped backward. He planted his hands on his hips and stared at her, a stormy expression on his face.

"You fired Ethel?" he roared. "What in the hell for? You didn't even give her a chance. Do you know how hard it is to find a housekeeper?"

"I don't want a housekeeper," Courtney said, none too quietly. "If you had bothered to ask me, I would have told you that. I will take care of our children and our home. Me. Not some descendent of a Sumo wrestler."

"I don't want you working so hard," Luke shouted. "This house is too big for you to handle alone. You've got better things to do with your time."

"Oh? Like what? You tell me, Luke, like what?"

"Being a wife and mother, dammit!"

"Exactly. And that's part of my job, tending to this home."

"No."

"Listen to me, Luke," she said tightly. "I didn't argue when you took over everything this past month. I went along with teenagers plowing through my personal possessions, and a real estate agent who acted as though I didn't have a brain in my head. The list goes on and on of the things I did your way rather than create a hassle. But not this time. I won't have a housekeeper here whom I don't want. I absolutely refuse."

"Took over everything?" he repeated, his voice ominously low. "You view what I did as taking over?"

"You never discussed anything. You just did it. I have a mind, a voice, opinions."

"I was trying to help you, relieve you of burdens. You make me sound like a damn dictator."

"Oh, Luke," she said, sighing. "I appreciate everything you did. But don't you see? You're not leaving me anything."

"You're not a maid!"

"No, I'm a wife, a mother, a homemaker. That's who I am, what I am. That's what brings me infinite joy. Let me do what I do best."

"I don't believe this," he said, shaking his head. "I'm trying to be a decent man, a good husband and father, and you're flinging all my efforts back into my face. I was ridding you of burdensome responsibilities. But you didn't like that, apparently. What is it with you, Courtney? Do you always have to be the one in charge, in control?"

"No. That's a terrible thing to say."

"Yeah, well, accusing me of taking over your life isn't exactly sweetness and light. Hell, I'll never know where I stand with you. What's the plan? You make another one of your damn lists to inform me what areas of your life I have some say in?"

"Luke, that's enough."

"You're right about that, lady," he said, spinning around and starting for the door.

"Where are you going?"

"For a walk." He roughly slammed the door closed behind him.

"Oh, damn," Courtney said as tears sprang to her eyes. "Oh, damn, damn."

Somehow Courtney managed to plaster a smile on her face when she called the children to dinner. Luke, she told them, had had an emergency at work and had to go back to the office. She then glanced heavenward and asked forgiveness for her bold-faced lie. The meal seemed endless as she listened for Luke's return. Kevin retold his Disneyland adventures, and Courtney commented in all the right places.

She cleaned the kitchen, read stories to the children, gave them baths and tucked Jessica in her crib. There was no sign of Luke. After Kevin went to bed, Courtney wandered aimlessly around the large, quiet living room, replaying over and over in her mind the heated argument with Luke.

Be patient with him, Anne had said. Luke would give her the moon and the stars if he could. He loved her, Courtney didn't doubt that, but he was smothering her with kind deeds, not allowing her to do what she wanted to do. They'd talk it through, compromise, reach a workable agreement.

But they couldn't do that if Luke didn't come home.

Dear Lord, where was he? she wondered frantically. He was on foot. How long could a man walk around when he was mad as hell?

Suddenly a strange thudding noise sounded at the front door. Courtney moved cautiously forward.

"Yes?" she called.

"It's Luke," came the muffled reply. "Open up."

She flung open the door, then stared wide-eyed at what greeted her.

It wasn't Luke. It was two arms stretched around the biggest bouquet of California poppies imaginable. The flowers moved into the room, and Courtney scooted out of the way.

"Luke, what . . ." She slid her hands through the blossoms and pressed them aside to uncover his face.

"Hi," he said, grinning at her. "I brought you a flower. Or two."

"Right," she said, nodding slowly. Then she yelled, as Luke suddenly opened his arms and allowed the poppies to fall in a huge pile on the floor.

"Courtney," he said. His voice was low, his smile gone. "I'm so damn sorry. Everything I did for you I did out of love, but I screwed it up so badly. Piece by piece I was taking from you all the things that are important to you. My ego was blown to smithereens when I stormed out of here. I had tried to protect and care for you, and, by God, you were supposed to love every minute of it."

"Oh, Luke, I—"

"Then I saw the poppies growing wild in a field. I just stood there staring at them like an idiot. I went over in my mind that first day I met you, when you were going to shoot me dead with a wrench. I remembered your telling me that your poppies weren't weeds, they were golden meadows. You were so full of love, and your home rang with laughter. I think I started falling in love with you at that very moment."

Tears filled Courtney's eyes.

"Seeing the golden meadows," he went on, "where others see weeds is a gift. Making a home out of a house is a gift. Knowing how to love the way you do is a gift. I thought I was giving you more gifts by arranging the sale of your house, hiring a house-keeper, but I wasn't. I was taking, not giving. Taking away all that is you, who you are, the woman I love. Courtney . . ." His voice broke, and his green eyes shone with tears. "I brought you this golden meadow to beg your forgiveness. Let's start over. Okay? Oh, God, Courtney . . . please!"

She hurled herself into his arms and he held her so tightly, she could hardly breathe. She tilted her head back and gazed up at him.

"Oh, Luke," she said, "you *did* give to me. You gave me your love, laughter, your support and car-ing. You gave me you, and I love you so much. No, we're not starting over, we're going forward, having learned and grown. Thank you for my golden meadow. These are the most beautiful flowers I've ever been given."

Luke cradled her face in trembling hands and gazed at her with such love and tenderness that fresh tears sprang to Courtney's eyes. He circled her shoulders with his arm and turned off the light. Then they walked down the hall to their private place, their loving place, their place of ecstasy.

The moon slid from behind a cloud and shone brightly, casting a silvery luminescence over the liv-ing room. The poppies on the floor were transformed, shimmering with beauty, as though touched by a magic wand found only in a home filled with love.

THE EDITOR'S CORNER

This summer is going to be one of the best ever! That's not a weather forecast, but a reading report. There will be some very special publishing events you can look forward to that reach just beyond the regular LOVESWEPT fare—which, of course, is as wonderful as always. Alas, I'm limited by space, so I have to try to restrain my urge to describe these books in loving detail. (How I regret that brevity is not one of my virtues!)

During the first week of next month, a brilliant and heartwarming love story will appear in your bookstores—**NEVER LEAVE ME** by Margaret Pemberton. (This Bantam book may be housed in romance sections of some stores, general fiction of others. Do look for it or ask your bookseller to pull a copy for you. Trust me, this is a story you will *not* want to miss!) British, a mother of five, and a wonderfully stylish and talented storyteller, Margaret was first published by us in December 1985. That novel, **GODDESS,** was the compelling love story of Valentina, a mysterious young woman who became a legendary film star, and Vidal, the passionate, powerful, unattainable man who was her discoverer and director. This story often comes hauntingly to my mind. Now, in **NEVER LEAVE ME**, Margaret tells the equally haunting, yet quite different story of Lisette de Valmy, of her forbidden love and a secret that very nearly shatters her happiness. The man she will marry, Greg Derring, is nothing short of marvelous . . . and the climax of the book is so full of emotional richness and poignancy that I dare you to finish the story dry-eyed.

The following month you have an enormous, happy surprise—the zany, chilling, sexy **HOT ICE** by Nora Roberts. I bet you've loved Nora's more than forty romances during the last few years as much as I have. (Yes, we do love books published by our honorable competitors!) How were we so lucky that we got to publish a Nora Roberts book? Well, because what she is writing for us is outside the range of her Silhouette love stories. **HOT ICE** is a romantic suspense, a zesty adventure tale with a grand love story between an ice cream heiress, Whitney, and a criminal—a real, non-garden variety thief with plenty of street smarts—Doug. They're the sassiest, most delightful couple I've encountered since *Romancing The Stone* and the first episode

(continued)

of *Moonlighting*! In the back of **HOT ICE** you'll get an excerpt of Nora's next romantic suspense novel, **SACRED SINS,** an absolutely breathtaking tale, which will be published in December, on sale the first week of November.

THE DELANEY DYNASTY LIVES ON! In July we will distribute a free sampler to tease you unmercifully about the marvelous trilogy **THE DELANEYS OF KILLAROO,** which gives you the love stories of three dynamite ladies of the Australian branch of the Delaney family. But we won't torment you long, because the full works go on sale in early August. Of course these fabulous books were written by the ladies of **THE SHAMROCK TRINITY:** Kay Hooper, Iris Johansen, and Fayrene Preston.

I must rush along now so that, hopefully, I can tantalize you with a few words on the LOVESWEPTs for next month.

NOT A MARRYING MAN by Barbara Boswell, LOVE-SWEPT #194, reintroduces you to a shameless rogue you met briefly before, Sterne Lipton. (Remember him? He's the brother of the heroine of **LANDSLIDE VICTORY.**) Well, Sterne has more than met his match in Brynn Cassidy. When she finds out he's wagered a bundle on getting her into bed, she sets out to teach the ruthless bachelor a ruthless lesson. But soon both of them are wildly, madly, completely in love with one another . . . and in deep hot water. Funny, touching, **NOT A MARRYING MAN** is one more superb love story from Barbara, whose work never fails to delight.

I can't tell you what a pleasure it was for me to work on Sara Orwig's witty and wonderful, **WIND WARNING,** LOVE-SWEPT #195. Savannah Carson and Mike Smith crash into one another on boats in Lake Superior. Mike quite literally falls overboard for the lovely lady, too, but grave danger denies them the freedom to stay together. **WIND WARNING** should carry a cautionary label—its heroine and hero just might steal your heart.

Never, ever has a tent in the wilderness held a more exciting couple than in Hertha Schulze's **SOLID GOLD PROSPECT,** LOVESWEPT #196. Heroine Nita Holiday is a woman with whom each of us can readily identify as we learned so well in Hertha's first LOVESWEPT, **BEFORE AND AFTER,** because she's an avid romance reader. Mr. Right seems to her to have stepped right off the page of a LOVESWEPT when she sets eyes on Matt Lamartine. And

(continued)

Matt can scarcely tear himself away from the beguiling woman whose background is so different from his own that it shakes him right down to his toes. From New York to Chicago to the vast, romantic wilderness of Canada, Nita and Matt pursue passion . . . and the understanding that can make their love last forever. An utterly sensational romance.

As the New Year began some months ago I was thinking back over the years, remembering the writers with whom I've had long relationships. Among them, of course, is Sandra Brown whose warm friendship I have enjoyed as much as her superb professionalism. One of the many things I admire about Sandra is that she never rests on her laurels. She constantly challenges herself to achieve new writing goals— and all of us are the beneficiaries. In her next romance, **DEMON RUMM,** LOVESWEPT #197, you'll see another instance of how Sandra continues to expand her mastery of her craft for she writes this story exclusively from the hero's point-of-view. Rylan North is a famous, enigmatic, perfectionistic movie idol. Tapped to star as Demon Rumm, the late husband of the heroine, Kirsten, he moves into her house . . . her life . . . her very soul. Sultry and sensitive, this romance is one of Sandra's most memorable. A true keeper.

We hope you will be as excited as we are over the line-up of LOVESWEPTs and other novels that we've developed for a sensational summer of reading.

With every good wish,

Carolyn Nichols

Carolyn Nichols
  Editor
LOVESWEPT
Bantam Books, Inc.
666 Fifth Avenue
New York, NY 10103

*Heirs to a great dynasty, the Delaney
brothers were united by blood, united by
devotion to their rugged land . . . and
known far and wide as*

THE SHAMROCK
TRINITY

Bantam's bestselling LOVESWEPT romance line built its reputation on quality and innovation. Now, a remarkable and unique
event in romance publishing comes from the same source: THE
SHAMROCK TRINITY, three daringly original novels written by
three of the most successful women's romance writers today. Kay
Hooper, Iris Johansen, and Fayrene Preston have created a trio
of books that are dynamite love stories bursting with strong,
fascinating male and female characters, deeply sensual love scenes,
the humor for which LOVESWEPT is famous, and a deliciously
fresh approach to romance writing.

*THE SHAMROCK TRINITY—Burke, York, and
Rafe: Powerful men . . . rakes and charmers . . .
they needed only love to make their lives complete.*

☐ *RAFE, THE MAVERICK by Kay Hooper*

Rafe Delaney was a heartbreaker whose ebony eyes held laughing
devils and whose lilting voice could charm any lady—or any
horse—until a stallion named Diablo left him in the dust. It took
Maggie O'Riley to work her magic on the impossible horse . . .
and on his bold owner. Maggie's grace and strength made Rafe
yearn to share the raw beauty of his land with her, to teach her
the exquisite pleasure of yielding to the heat inside her. Maggie
was stirred by Rafe's passion, but would his reputation and her
ambition keep their kindred spirits apart?   (21786 • $2.50)

LOVESWEPT

☐ *YORK, THE RENEGADE by Iris Johansen*

Some men were made to fight dragons, Sierra Smith thought when she first met York Delaney. The rebel brother had roamed the world for years before calling the rough mining town of Hell's Bluff home. Now, the spirited young woman who'd penetrated this renegade's paradise had awakened a savage and tender possessiveness in York: something he never expected to find in himself. Sierra had known loneliness and isolation too—enough to realize that York's restlessness had only to do with finding a place to belong. Could she convince him that love was such a place, that the refuge he'd always sought was in her arms?

(21787 • $2.50)

☐ *BURKE, THE KINGPIN by Fayrene Preston*

Cara Winston appeared as a fantasy, racing on horseback to catch the day's last light—her silver hair glistening, her dress the color of the Arizona sunset . . . and Burke Delaney wanted her. She was on his horse, on his land: she would have to belong to him too. But Cara was quicksilver, impossible to hold, a wild creature whose scent was midnight flowers and sweet grass. Burke had always taken what he wanted, by willing it or fighting for it; Cara cherished her freedom and refused to believe his love would last. Could he make her see he'd captured her to have and hold forever?

(21788 • $2.50)